A Prophecies of Angels and
Demons Novella

Light

Book 2.5

CASSANDRA ASTON

For those who loved Romeo and Juliet, this one's for you

CONTENTS AND TRIGGER WARNINGS

This book is a work of fiction. No part of this book should be construed as true or accurate; no people or animals were harmed in the creation of this story. Light is intended for mature readers and recommends 18+. Mature content and triggers are listed below.

Descriptions of torture and death

Descriptions of family tragedy and mental and physical torture

References to war, human suffering and death

Necromancy and reincarnation

Biblical and other related references

References to angels, demons, heaven, hell, and consequences for human actions

Explicit language

Witches, magic, and other magical, fantastical beings

CONTENTS

CHAPTER 1

Gabriel

A cheer rose, setting Gabriel's teeth grinding together. He didn't begrudge them their happiness. In truth, he longed for his own contentment. That Uriel had found his mate after so long meant hope was not lost.

It also meant he was the last. The last of seventeen-thousand, seven hundred, seventy-seven siblings to find his analogous umbra. His other half. The piece of him which had been stolen several millennia ago.

He blinked in the bright glare surrounding him, so at odds with his mood. Alaxia was never devoid of light, a fact that grated on his nerves. The pearlescent glow refracting off every surface was enough to frequently drive him down to the mortal plane.

Another cheer sounded as trumpets blared.

Dina approached, clapping Gabriel's shoulder. "I'd begun to lose faith we'd see the day dear Uriel found his soulmate," she laughed.

Gabriel bit his tongue to stop the grinding he knew Dina would hear, even over the raucous crowd of celebratory seraphim.

Her gaze darted down to the fists balled at his sides, and her smile fell. "You will find your analogous umbra when Father deems it so, brother."

He worked his tongue between sharp teeth, relishing the pain of each slice of flesh, saying nothing. He watched Uriel and his mate clasp hands, bowing their heads until they touched as they drank each other in, melding their souls into one.

A new ache cleaved through him, bringing hollowness with it. He felt the absence of that vital part of his being. Where a soul should have been, only a shadow of it existed—a fraction of what once was.

Had he never known what it was to be whole, he might not begrudge the humans. But once, his soul had sung with the rightness of being complete, and like a phantom limb, the loss haunted him. When it was ripped in two, it was torture like nothing he'd ever known. It was meant to be. It was a punishment, after all.

"Your other half is out there," Dina tried again.

Gabriel narrowed his gaze on the faintly glowing circle just above her head. "What would you know of my suffering? You were one of the first."

Dina's white brow drew down over opalescent, swirling eyes. She glanced away, her gaze resting on Uriel and his Naphil, Henry. "Is the wait not worth the prize?"

Suddenly, the brightness and joy encircling him were too much. Gabriel spread his wings, forcing Dina to step back as he launched into the air, sailing over pearly gates to the edge of Alaxia's border, and continued down, dropping to the Earthly plane.

Cream ankle-high boots solidified on his feet as they met the ground. His shoulders twitched, dissolving his wings into a white tailored overcoat, tight at the waist but loose as it fell down the backs of his calves.

He pulled a tan top hat down low over his brow and strolled confidently along the cobbled street, avoiding the gazes of the gentry as they passed.

It was not yet dark, but he would rather be here among the humans who had taken so much from him than up there amongst the revelers.

He was in a mood to kill something.

Stepping under a sign that read *Bull and Butcher,* he pulled his top hat from his head, tucking it under one arm. A man behind the bar, ruddy-faced and glowering, looked up from where he wiped a dirty rag over darkly stained wood.

"Club steak's on to'nite, and ya buy a pint or yer out," he called and resumed wiping down the counter.

Gabriel glanced around the room, finding it sufficiently packed. The Bull and Butcher was a central hub of gossip on the high street; the sooner he could be about his business this night, the better.

Settling onto a stool at the bar, he slid his hat into the empty chair beside him, giving a rosy-cheeked woman a look that might have sent others running. Her crimson-dipped smile faltered when their eyes met, and he let just a bit of the rage in his dark eyes show.

They were unusual for his kind. Where many of his siblings had eyes of silver or gold, his were nearly black. A portent of some dark future, he often thought, but Dina said it was the absence of light, stripped away when his soul had been wrenched in two. She speculated he'd lost more than the others. Why, only Father knew.

The woman stumbled into a man behind her, mumbling apologies as she made her hasty retreat. Better for her if she avoided him. Better for them all.

The barman set a pint of ale in front of Gabriel, but his attention was drawn to the pub door as it was jostled open. He tracked two men in uniform as they moved through the room, settling into chairs in a far dark corner.

These were just the sort of men Gabriel was looking for. Over the din, he tuned his ears to their voices, blocking out the boisterous patrons singing along to a bawdy tune.

"Three dead," the first uniformed man said.

"Mart's again?" the second man asked.

"Wasn't the pox. Mart's claimin' wild beasts."

"Dollymop never did shoot us straight."

"What then?"

"Damfino."

Gabriel slid his stool back, reaching for his hat. The only wild beasts terrorizing London streets were the nasdaqu-ush. He strode for the door, placing it atop his head.

"Gotta pay fer that!" the barman shouted behind him.

Scowling, he turned, setting two coins on the counter—more than enough to pay for a meal and a pint. The barman nodded and turned away, saying nothing about the food he'd not yet been served.

It was just as well—he wouldn't have eaten it.

Streaks of orange slid between narrow gaps in buildings, lighting his path as he turned onto Mill Street and lengthened his stride. He could have moved through air to arrive in moments, but it would not be dark for some time, and though he was loath to admit it, he liked the filthy cobbled streets of South London.

It was alive with pain and suffering in a manner he knew too well. The stench of misery and loss clung to the air, coating his skin. He felt a quiet companionship among those who understood him in a way his brethren never would.

Dina may have been right when she surmised he had lost more of his soul than the other seraphim.

If it was meant as a punishment for their dalliances with humans all those centuries ago, why had he been dealt the worst blow? He'd never known the touch of a mortal, never given in to the temptations of human flesh.

He stopped, peering up at the shanty of a building leaning against its neighbor. It was the perfect place for the nasdaqu-ush to hunt. Mere steps from the Thames and bordered on two sides by dark alcoves, the creatures could easily slip in and out unseen.

Red rimmed the horizon, painting the landscape in shades of gray. It was nearly time.

Gabriel knocked.

Slowly, the door creaked open, revealing a sallow face framed in dark, greasy curls. Mart's sharp eyes trailed down Gabriel's pristine breeches and back up. A wide grin split her face, exposing cracked, yellow teeth.

"What can I do you for ya this eve, kind sir?"

"I'd like a room."

CHAPTER 2

Gabriel

Gabriel leaned against the window frame of his rented room. Outside, the night was warm. Sticky heat pressed against the cool of the building's aged walls as he trailed his gaze over the dark nooks and crannies below.

A boy, not yet twelve, worked methodically down the street, lighting each hanging lantern. He made his way toward the building, stopping at each to relight his wick before raising it on an extended pole. As he drew nearer, the path lit, illuminating darkened corners.

A light knock caught Gabriel momentarily by surprise. He stood, cracking the door. Mart stared up at him, her watery eyes glinting.

"I'll be sendin' my best girl in, sir. Do ya have a preference? I got girls of all shapes 'n sizes. Ya won't be disappointed."

Gabriel grimaced. "I'll only require the room. Thank you."

Mart's eyes narrowed. "There'll be no foul deeds done here, sir. The room's fur pleasure only."

Gabriel nodded, pulling five gold coins out. "Nothing untoward will happen; I assure you."

Her mouth fell slack as she accepted his coin. It was far too large a sum for the establishment, but it would ensure he was undisturbed for the rest of the evening.

He glanced over his shoulder, back to the street below. She said something else, but he wasn't listening. The boy was gone. Lit lanterns stopped just outside her building. The damned woman had distracted him.

"Excuse me, I forgot my coat. I'll return momentarily." He pushed the door wide, stepping around Mart, and moved swiftly down the hall. Tuning out the crude sounds and muffled banging of furniture against walls inside, he listened.

There. A body cutting through the air, displacing the natural order of things with its unnatural presence. He stilled, hand on the door. It was unusually fast. To capture it, he could not simply walk out and face it.

Moving through space with so many humans present was a risk, but one he would take to rid the streets of another vile being. He dissolved into dust and shifted through the air to the place the creature would be in seconds. Materializing with Dina's flaming sword in hand, he sliced through a body as it solidified on the blade.

Eyes of gold and amber rounded in surprise before the nasdaqu-ush slid down steel, hanging limply against the pommel.

He placed both hands on the vile thing, returning it to the dust from whence it came. Bits of ash floated to the ground, the only evidence it had been there.

Flicking his hand, he cast blue fire along his fingers, running them down the sword, cleansing it of the creature's remains, and smothering the flame before sheathing it beneath his camouflaged wings.

Glancing around the darkened street, he saw a form crumpled against a dark wall.

Crossing, he stooped and pressed two fingers against the boy's neck. Nothing. He lifted the lad's chin, exposing torn flesh. Although Sanura's goal was to wipe the Gavras line from the Earth, she never missed an opportunity to add to her ever-expanding army. It would be better not to leave a body behind for her to use.

He laid both hands on the boy, dissolving his form to dust—one less creature to hunt.

CHAPTER 3

Adalaide

Adalaide pressed the worn leather journal against her chest, sighing. Tonight, as with many nights, she had found herself on the roof, seeking redemption from the heavens. It had been eight years, but the burden she carried for her crimes weighed no less heavily on her soul than it had the day she'd committed the offenses.

It had been self-defense. An accident. But it had left her an orphan at sixteen.

Lifting her skirts, she stood and moved to the edge, glancing down at the street below. It was pitch dark, the only light the faint glow of street lanterns sparsely illuminating the winding path.

Leaning back, Adalaide gripped the roof's overhanging ledge and stretched her head upward to take in the night sky. Millions of tiny lights glittered and sparkled in some happy parody of a beautiful night.

But there was nothing beautiful about life anymore.

A breeze trailed along the back of her neck, sending goose pimples rippling over her skin. It was unseasonably warm, and the air spoke of grim foreboding. Something dangerous was coming.

Another featherlight breeze ruffled her raven curls, and apprehension slid down her spine. This was more than a premonition of dark deeds to come. It was a warning—an immediate one.

Adalaide closed her eyes, opening her third eye, and sent it wafting on the phantom wind. She let it drift toward the thing that set her nerves on edge. Her third eyesight swam lazily over building tops, stretching further than it had traveled before. It stopped, hovering far to the left where the Thames dipped through Jacob's Island, catching the poorest residents' filth and waste. A blue haze settled there, forming the soft shape of an arrow. It pointed downriver.

She tried to press her sight toward the arrow, but it dissipated, going no further. What did it mean?

Her abilities had arrived early and by sixteen, she was aware of their magnitude. A formidable energy lived within her, powered her, like one of Alessandro Volta's strange inventions, lighting her up.

Each day, she discovered new gifts. But as time passed, she became more convinced she was the only one of her kind. Her father had had exceptional abilities, made greater by the use of wicked magic and the amulet she now wore, but his gifts, even amplified, paled in comparison to hers.

A new breeze—hot this time—drifted by, warning her of approaching danger.

Squeezing her eyes shut, she cast her third eyesight around her in a circle and jolted as the blue haze, previously on the other side of town, beat a path toward her at a rapid pace.

Blinking her lids open, she backed up, sending both hands to her sides, and lifted herself into the air, maneuvering out over the ground. She gave the air magic a little push and angled herself into the window on the third floor of her townhouse.

Whirling as her feet met the carpet, she slammed the window down and bolted it shut.

She closed her eyes once, confirming the blue was nearly there. It was blocks away, moving faster than any creature she'd yet encountered. She ran to the first floor and slid the deadbolt into place.

Heart racing, she sagged against the door. The creature was coming for her. She knew it with every fiber of her being.

And it wasn't the first.

She'd encountered dozens of the strange creatures since her gifts had awoken. Once, she'd believed them to be of her father's making, but now that he was gone, she knew they were something else.

Not demons—the dark, wispy forms who stalked through the night seeking debauchery and malicious intent. These seemed bent on one purpose. She could only assume it was some natural phenomenon. Nature demanded balance, after all, and she was an unnatural thing, too powerful for this world.

Or perhaps it was because her soul was tarnished, marred by the death of her mother and father. Maybe they were angels coming to exact revenge against her wickedness.

Something hard smacked the wood at her back, reverberating against it, making her jump back.

Steadying her breathing, she raised both hands, casting them in a vibrant blue hue. Flames licked down her fingers, trailing along her arms. Wrestling her wild flames into submission took all her focus, but they were highly effective against the yellow-eyed creatures who hunted her.

The door shook again, a crack forming along the center.

It was strong. Stronger than the others she'd encountered. Another loud crack and the wood splintered straight up the middle.

She widened her stance, preparing.

A snap that sounded her demise split the door in two, and a woman with hair the color of blood materialized inside her foyer. She brushed splinters of wood from her arms, looking Adalaide up and down before ruby lips split into a wide grin.

11

"You've been more difficult to kill than expected." The words dripped like honey from her perfect mouth. There was something otherworldly about her, and the power she exuded was intoxicating, drawing Adalaide in and sweeping her up in a warm embrace.

She swayed on her feet, caught in some imaginary tune that beckoned her to come closer. Shaking her head, Adalaide raised her hands, pulling at the ember of power buried in her chest, and the room glowed, suffused in sapphire blue.

The woman's red hair shook as she took in Adalaide's flame and tsked. "Not bad," she purred, "but in my time, we were gods. How the line has been diluted."

Adalaide struggled to make sense of the words rolling off the woman's tongue in an accent she couldn't place. "Why have you come?" she managed to ask.

The woman laughed, a musical sound that threatened to break Adalaide's tenuous grip on control.

"I've come to kill you."

The woman's words cleared some of the fog in Adalaide's mind, and she called on her air magic to cast herself in a bubble that would block the sound of her melodic voice.

The moment the world went silent, she drew in a deep breath, her mind clearing.

Her only chance would be to move the fight outdoors, where she could use air magic. She darted a glance through the split door to the darkness beyond. The woman hadn't attacked yet. She was waiting for something. Or... *looking* for something.

As if in answer to her unspoken question, the amulet pressed against her breast warmed and pulsed.

Something in the woman's yellow eyes changed, and Adalaide knew she'd felt its presence, too.

Wasting no more time, she dropped her air bubble and flung flaming arrows at the woman. The woman darted faster than Adalaide could track, clearing a path to the door.

Adalaide dived for it, crying out as the woman's taloned nail scraped her skin, tearing fabric and slicing a sharp line down her arm. She cleared the door and thrust her hands to the ground, pressing all her energy into the movement.

She shot into the sky, and her stomach dipped as the ground disappeared below. "Blast it!" she cried as she began her descent.

She pressed her hands against her sides and pulled at the ember in her chest, forcing herself back up and angled her hands until she drifted toward her townhouse's roof. The woman's crimson hair streaked through the door of her townhouse, and within moments, she was on the roof, swiping for Adalaide's ankles.

Adalaide let out a shrill cry, pushing off the rooftop. Soon, she was perilously high; with nothing to levitate over, she began another rapid descent.

The yellow-eyed woman trailed her motion to the street and raced back down to meet her.

Adalaide gave another powerful push of air magic and collapsed onto the roof of the adjacent building, panting, and pressed her hand to her shoulder where she'd been cut.

The woman shouted something and began her assault on the door of the building Adalaide was now perched atop. Adalaide leaned against the ledge, her heart galloping. With the woman's speed, she could keep this up all night, and Adalaide would run out of energy before long.

She needed a new plan.

CHAPTER 4

Gabriel

Gabriel hadn't imagined it. There *had* been a second creature. It was trailing the Thames, headed south, when suddenly, it changed direction, moving toward the posh district. Nasdaqu-ush avoided brightly lit parts of the city. It could only be headed to its lair.

Perhaps he could catch the lot of them and wipe the city's entire infestation out in one night.

He followed its stale breeze, the scent of carrion and death heavy. It wasn't a nasdaqu-ush at all. He was on the trail of their maker. The night had taken a turn for the better.

He leapt from the ground, dissolving into dust, and rode its wake. When the creature halted, he materialized, freezing at the scene before him.

A Naphil. His breath caught. It was the first he'd encountered in decades. She was levitating high above him and landed on a rooftop just as a red-haired woman beat her fists into the door of the townhouse.

Sanura.

He dropped to the ground behind her, drawing his sword. "I've waited a long time for this moment," he said, running a blue-hued flinger along the blade.

Sanura spun, eyes going wide.

He charged forward, but she wasted no time darting away and disappearing into the darkness. Growling, he raced after her, but he was not as fast as she was, and in moments, she had disappeared, leaving no trail for him to follow.

Some invisible force pulled him, turning him around, back to the Naphil. He didn't have time for the distraction. Didn't have the energy to go back and be disappointed again.

It was the closest he'd come to catching Sanura in over a century. How she'd evaded them for so long was a mystery. If he let her escape now, it could be another hundred years before he had this chance again.

He pivoted on his toes, leaping into the night sky, and moved in the direction he'd seen her go. Flying was always faster than any other mode of travel for him, but somehow, it wasn't fast enough.

He left the city, blinking in the inky dark of a moonless night. She may be right below him and he would be blind to her presence. Perhaps she'd turned back, intent on finishing what she'd started. It was the lie he told himself to justify the sweep he made as he circled back.

The Naphil was on the roof, scanning the sky. She wouldn't see him, though. He was dust and air and nothing more. She continued searching, trailing her gaze across the expanse of darkness as if *he* were what she sought and not Sanura.

For Sanura to come out of hiding was concerning. What about this girl was important enough that Sanura would risk it?

The answer struck him: she was a Gavras, a member of the line who had killed Sanura centuries ago. It meant she was marked for death.

He swept by once more, solidifying as he touched down on a rooftop far enough away that she would not see him, even with her enhanced Nephilim vision.

After centuries of chasing her, he finally had the upper hand. Sanura would be back to kill this woman, and when she came, he would be waiting.

CHAPTER 5

Adalaide

When Adalaide was certain the woman and the other creature who had appeared to chase her off would not return, she gave one last push of magic and levitated to the ground.

She trudged up the steps, dragging her tired limbs through the broken door, and slumped into a chair in her foyer. Sighing heavily, she stared at the gaping entryway. She would need to find a temporary fix before resting.

Hefting her sore body out of the chair, she went to the guest room at the front of the house and eyed the empty armoire in the room's corner. It was heavy and would do the trick for the night.

With her last bit of energy, she sent a gust of air magic under the object and pushed it roughly through the room. In the doorframe, she shoved her shoulder into the wood, wedging it sideways, and gave another push of magic until it was scraping over wooden floors and through the foyer.

She surveyed her work, shaking her head. It needed something extra. Cracking her knuckles, she dug deep, finding the well of power lying at the center of her chest and wove the wards that would hold the object in place for the night.

Standing back, she swayed on her feet, exhaustion overtaking her. Opting for the guest room on the first floor over dragging herself above stairs, she collapsed onto the soft white duvet and closed her eyes.

CHAPTER 6

Gabriel

Gabriel materialized in her room and stifled a snort. The woman had collapsed on a large four-poster bed, landing face down, fully clothed, her shoes poking over the edge. He moved to the side of the bed, watching the slow rise and fall of her back as she sunk further into the fluffy bedding. *Alive then.*

"Mother. No... Please. No." she murmured into the bedding. A line of drool pooled in her blankets, and as she turned her head, it smeared across her cheek.

Moving around the bed, he crossed his arms, studying full pouting lips as she continued to mumble into the blankets.

She was attractive—for a human.

Her raven brows were perfectly sculpted over pale lids fringed in thick black lashes. A small, somewhat pointed nose rose delicately from her face, and tiny, nearly invisible freckles were dusted over it. A pink top lip forming a perfect bow rested on a fuller bottom lip, and they were turned down as if, even in sleep, life disappointed her.

He understood the feeling.

Her pale cheeks held the faintest flush, coloring them a rosy hue. Not painted. Natural. Flushed from the exertions of the evening.

She mumbled again, and he froze when her eyes flew open and startlingly blue irises met his. They were piercing in their intensity, and something stirred in his chest.

Hope, he thought. *No*. He would not give in to that dangerous emotion. Hope was a thing that had died long ago for him.

Her eyes fell closed as she said, "That's not a fair price for lace at all."

His immediate relief at not being discovered startled another laugh out of him. Was she dreaming of haggling for lace?

He had resolved to stay the night and wait for Sanura to return, but Sanura was calculating. She would not be back tonight. He knew it but couldn't make himself leave. Backing up, he settled into a chair in the room's corner.

Maintaining his human facade, he let his wings drape like coattails beneath him as he sat. It was uncomfortable and left him feeling weak and exposed, but an irrational fear of being discovered in his true form left him paralyzed in this one.

As he settled in, preparing for any threat, his gaze repeatedly found its way to the woman draped over the bed; the space in his chest he tried to ignore hummed a merry tune.

The night would be long indeed.

Gabriel's gaze trailed to the window—noting the glimmer of pre-dawn light fighting the dark to wash the world in its bright glaze—as he stood.

After the night's exertions, the Naphil may not rise for hours, but Sanura would be safely tucked away by now, preparing her mortal shell for its period of stasis. Although she was not a true nasdaqu-ush, the magic she'd used all those years ago to resurrect her body meant she could only walk the Earth at night. The woman, still drooling into her pillow, would be safe for the day.

He turned from the room, glancing back only once. Something sharp stabbed his chest moments before he left the mortal plane.

When he landed in Alaxia, the feeling dissipated, and he sighed with relief. Some physical manifestation of nearing completion of his mission, no doubt. Nothing to trouble himself over.

Striding through gilded halls, he stopped outside the arched door of his closest sibling and cleared his throat.

"Enter," Aaron said from within.

Gabriel stepped through the door, glancing around the starkly white marble room. "Is Dina in?"

Aaron stood from where he'd been reclining in a white tufted chair, setting a book on the alabaster marble table beside him, and crossed the room to clasp Gabriel's arm.

He was struck by the similarities between Aaron and the Naphil he'd met last night. He should have known she was of the Gavras line the moment he laid eyes on her. They were different, of course, separated by thousands of years, but her piercing blue eyes, dark hair, and tall stature were only a few of the things that made their connection unmistakable.

"She has been called to Assyria once more."

"I believe the humans call it Syria now," Gabriel said, chuckling.

Aaron's dark brows drew down, furrowing. "As you say, brother. The death toll swells by the day. She is sorely needed. I only wish I could go with her."

Gabriel nodded. "I'll see myself out," he said, turning to leave Dina and Aaron's room.

"Dina told me of your pain," Aaron said, halting Gabriel in the arched doorway. "Your analogous umbra is out there, brother."

Gabriel swallowed. Discussing these matters with Dina was one thing, but discussing them with the human mate she'd found centuries ago was another. His eyes narrowed as he glanced down at Aaron's hand resting on his biceps.

He backed up, stepping out of Aaron's reach. "I'll tell Dina you long for her return."

Aaron's lips pursed, but he said nothing, pacing away from Gabriel and returning to his chair beside a massive wall of books.

Gabriel didn't look back as he stepped into the hall, leaving Dina's Naphil to whatever enjoyment he found while Dina was away.

CHAPTER 7

Gabriel

Gabriel dropped beside his sister, crossing his arms over his chest. From high on this rocky peak, it was easy to take in the beauty of their Father's might, overlooking the petty squabbles of humans who sought to paint the land in death and despair.

A thunderous boom rent the air, disturbing its peace. It was followed by three more; shouts and screams became a wailing cacophony, destroying the sense of calm.

"Aaron misses you," Gabriel said into the moment of silence as Dina paused time.

Her swirling opalescent eyes fell on him, a soft smile forming at the edges of her mouth. "As I do him. Have you come to aid me?"

He shook his head. "I have found Sanura."

Dina started, the moment in time rupturing as she turned to face him. Over the sounds of metal clashing and cannon booms, she said, "Have you told Uriel?"

"It's too soon for him to be parted from his analogous umbra. I've come for your help."

Dina frowned. "My hands are quite full here." She waved a hand toward the battle raging below.

"We change the world when we rid it of her. No more nasdaqu-ush. Think of it, Dina."

Dina was silent, watching as one ship sank beneath the waves and another glided forward, taking its place.

There were no demons present, only humans battling for power and dominance. Dina could do nothing for them, and she knew it. He could tell by the set of her jaw as she watched them kill one another.

"Tonight," she said, not looking at him. "I assume you have a plan."

"Thank you."

She glanced down at his fingers resting on her bare skin. "I would do anything for you, brother."

CHAPTER 8

Adalaide

Adalaide sat up, wiping crusted drool from her cheek. The room was bright—mid-day sun refracting off a floor-length mirror in the corner, streaking warm yellow light over her bed.

She groaned, pulling at the pins stabbing her skull, and freed her dark locks. She rubbed her fingers through her scalp, massaging the tender places. Sleeping with her hair pinned up had been a bad idea.

A sharp pain digging into her hip reminded her she'd also slept in her corset. It was a testament to just how drained she'd been that she hadn't fought the torturous contraption to remove it before passing out.

Shoes pinched her bound toes as she slid out of bed, and she groaned again. It was bad enough she had to bind herself in them all day, but to sleep the entire night in them was abuse.

She bent down, untying the lace of her boots and slipped stockinged feet free, sighing. She lifted her skirts, finding the edge of her stockings, and rolled them down.

On bare feet, she padded out of the room and up the stairs to the third floor, slipping inside her room. It was imperative she call on Arthur to replace her door before night, and she would need to retrieve the leather journal she'd dropped on the roof, but for the moment, she could take comfort in the freeing sensation of being unbound.

Undoing the buttons on her blouse, she pulled it loose and made quick work of unlacing the corset, which had been specially designed to get in and out of without the trouble of a maid.

She slid them off, laying them over a vanity table in the room's corner, and shimmied out of her skirts. When she was free of all her clothing, she dropped onto her bed and sighed contentedly.

It was unheard of for a lady of her standing to go about naked as a newborn, but feeling the rush of air that ran over pebbling skin—telling her stories of the day—was her favorite state of being.

It was a secret the good people of London would be truly scandalized by, but Adalaide Graves often slept in the nude.

She lay for a moment, staring up at the ceiling, stretching her long limbs like a cat. Each toe spread wide, and her fingers splayed overhead as she watched sunlight filtering over bare skin. Its warmth heated the ember in her chest, refilling some of the energy she'd drained the night before.

Letting her mind drift, she thought back to the events of the evening. The woman, not a witch as she'd first thought, had an air of something unique.

When Adalaide crossed paths with other witches, her own gifts recognized whichever of theirs was strongest. Sometimes, she could feel more than one gift, and once, she'd met a witch with three, but never all four elemental gifts like herself. The woman last night was powerful, but none of Adalaide's gifts had responded when she had appeared in her foyer.

And Adalaide would be dead now if not for the man. Man wasn't the right word. He'd felt like *her*.

Her senses had gone haywire when he appeared. It was as if he had materialized from nothing. But unlike the night-creatures or even the other witches who displaced the world around them, he was a part of it. Molded from the very fabric of existence.

She had been so distracted by his appearance that she'd forgotten to use her third eye to get a better look at him. Still, there had been a feeling. Something she couldn't put words to.

She touched a finger to her bare chest, remembering how her ember had pulsed as if to say, *good day friend*.

The old grandfather clock downstairs chimed the third hour. If she hoped to ward the house and fix the door before nightfall, she had no more time to waste.

CHAPTER 9

Gabriel

Gabriel made a fifth circle and landed on the adjacent roof to the Naphil's home.

Workers had replaced the door, and the woman had spent the better part of the afternoon warding it with various spells. Her magic was powerful for a Nephilim. Something uncomfortable twisted in his chest. *He* had strong magic, the strongest of all his siblings. Possibly even enough to rival the Fallen.

His other half would be equally powerful when compared with her kind.

"No," he said the word aloud as if giving voice to it could deter the tiny ember attempting to take root. He would not let that feeling grow again, only to have his hope dashed against the rocks of despair when it turned out she was not his. Being Nephilim did not make her *his*. And being of the Gavras line marked her for premature death.

If she died... or rejected him...

"No," he said again, shaking his head to put more emphasis on the word. He would not become like Aniel, lost forever to his grief.

Once he had rejoiced in a day when his two halves would reunite. Once he had looked upon every born Naphil with hope.

After so many millennia, that hope was dead.

The woman, Miss Graves, the workers called her, took a bite of cookie and set it back on the plate beside her. She had dragged a small table and chair out onto the footway and sat with a leather journal and cookies, weaving spells throughout the early afternoon.

From his vantage point, there wasn't a bare patch of stone or glass. Whether it would be strong enough to keep out Sanura was a different matter.

Gabriel smirked as she jumped up from her seat, dusting crumbs down a deep burgundy skirt. They fell to the cobbled sidewalk as she cursed the crumbs in a very unladylike manner and glared at the offending cookie.

She was taller than he'd first thought. It was more noticeable now as she stood beside the low table, brushing out her skirts. Her dark hair, though bound, was loosely done, and a knot of curls rested against her shoulder rather than being secured beneath a bonnet, as was expected when a lady was out of doors.

Miss Graves's journal ruffled in the wind, and the pages turned several times. She sat cursing again and began flipping through them.

He snorted as she flicked furiously, mumbling more curses under her breath. Not ladylike at all.

The air shifted as Dina landed silently beside him, and he schooled his features into blank indifference.

"A Naphil," she breathed.

He glanced sideways at her. "Don't."

"Gabriel, you must know what this means."

"I said *don't*."

Dina opened her mouth, but, seeing his expression, closed it.

They watched in silence as she continued flipping pages. When she had finished her work, the woman stuffed the leather journal under her arm and pulled the chair behind her, going into her townhouse.

Dina eyed him as if she wanted to say more, but her lips remained sealed as her gaze darted between Gabriel and the woman struggling with the table below.

When she was inside, her door locked, they moved to the street, checking her spells.

"The work is good. These are powerful wards."

Gabriel nodded, sending a soft rush of air at the door. It was absorbed, strengthening the magic. "Smart."

Dina rested a hand on his shoulder. "It could be that—"

"I watched her cast these spells. She knew Sanura was a witch and cast them intending to absorb magic."

"That may be, but it doesn't mean—"

Gabriel's teeth ground together. This time, he didn't hide the sound, and Dina flinched back. "In three thousand years, we've never caught Sanura. In three thousand years, she's killed every human in your line. If this woman is the last, she's the only thing standing between Sanura and her revenge. Do you believe we will stop her this time when we've failed so many times before?"

The words had struck a blow, and Dina stumbled back as if they were a physical one.

Gabriel sucked in a breath. "Dina, I'm sorry."

She shook her head, the overcoat she'd been wearing rippling between wings and a coat before she got the illusion under control.

"That was cruel. I beg your pardon."

Her hair swayed as she twisted her head from side to side. "Though I only ever knew the love of a mother once, I've loved them all. All the children of my line. I know you suffer, and more than that, you fear, but you cannot fight what Father prescribed. Would it not be worse to let her meet her end before you've had a chance to become one?"

Something cold settled in Gabriel's chest. "She may not be mine." The words were a whisper.

"Who else could she belong to?"

The truth of Dina's words sent fear shooting through him. Who else, indeed?

CHAPTER 10

Adalaide

Adalaide set her journal down on the side table and fell onto the stiff cushion of her sofa. It was dark, the grandfather clock having just rung the ninth hour. She had hoped whatever events would unfold this night would do so early enough that she would not sit for hours waiting or, worse, fall asleep and be murdered right there on her couch.

A soft knock at the door startled her.

Would the red-haired woman knock? Anything was possible. Perhaps it was a ploy to weaken her defenses.

She sat, listening for the sounds that might warn of impending danger. It was silent. So silent, she knew it was unnatural.

Closing her eyes, she opened her third eye, sending it down the hall to the door, and pushed it through the wards—only to encounter a light so blindingly brilliant it sent her crashing backward in her seat, forcing her third eye closed; even so, the bright streaks persisted for several moments longer.

When her true vision recovered, she touched a hand to her head and felt something like a magical headache. It throbbed, but not in her skull, exactly.

The soft knock at the door came again.

She stood, shuffling to the door. Whoever it was, it wasn't the witch with a blue haze from the night before.

"Who is it?"

"Miss Graves, may I speak with you?"

It was a man's voice, deep but polite.

She opened the door and took an involuntary step back. It was the man from the night before.

The warmth at the center of her chest gave a little jump, heating her breastbone. As before, her senses came alive, all her nerve endings sizzling, the ember in her chest straining forward.

"Good evening," she said a little breathlessly.

He was staring at her chest as if he could see the pulsing ember there.

He looked up. Their eyes met, and she marveled momentarily at the swirling depths of darkness in his before he moved, stepping effortlessly through her wards. He pressed her back against the wall, and her senses short-circuited as he crowded into her space, their bodies nearly touching.

"Someone is in your home," he whispered against her ear. "Stay here."

He backed up, giving her space, and she caught her breath, her heart galloping in her chest. She looked up, leaning her head back to gaze at the fierce cut of his jaw as his teeth ground together. A tiny thrill of terror shot through her; she couldn't tell if it was at the proximity of the man towering over her or his words.

His eyes were scanning the darkness beyond her, and she turned her head, searching for a danger that might be more threatening than the man who had just charged into her home.

"Don't move." As he said it, he vanished.

His words jarred her back into the present and she sucked in a breath, realizing she'd been holding it. A noise on the second floor startled her into action.

Searching desperately for a weapon and finding none, she dashed into the kitchen, grabbed her largest knife, and held it to her breast, sucking in sharp breaths as she listened for another sound.

Another loud bang sounded just overhead. Tightening her grip on the knife's handle, she raced up the stairs and slid to a halt in the hall. The dark outline of a hulking man was hunched over something on the floor.

Adalaide lunged forward, stabbing the blade into the tender place at his side where she knew it would inflict the most damage.

A guttural howl erupted from him as he reached for the blade handle and wrenched it out, tossing the knife to the floor.

Adalaide backed up, cold fear sliding down her spine as he stood. She spared a moment's glance at the glimmer of gold slicking the blade before the dark outline of her would-be attacker blocked the only light coming from a window at the other end of the hall.

She let out a small whimper as he turned and backed up another step. Her foot met air as she realized she'd backed up to the stairs too late. Rational thought left her as the world moved in slow motion, and she tipped backward, her whole body bending toward the ground.

As the room tilted, the man's face came into full view: it was the man who had rushed into her home. To save her? She couldn't be sure of his intentions, and now she would never know.

He lunged forward as the world caught up with her.

She was wrapped in warm arms, her head cradled gently against a broad chest, and a feeling of contented rightness stole through her entire being. In her whole life, no one had ever held her this way. Certainly not a man. A strange man. Alone with her. In her home.

The realization hit her the same moment it must have dawned on him, and she scrambled back as he released her, setting her on her feet.

She tipped her head back and stared up at the man who had saved her twice now, noticing the faintest glow along his silhouette.

"What... What are you?"

His full, dark lips parted in a smile. "I believe I am your soulmate."

CHAPTER II

Gabriel

He hadn't actually meant to say it. The words had just come out. He watched her staring at him blankly, shock or terror or some other emotion playing over her face, but he didn't know her well enough yet to discern it.

"I beg your pardon. What did you say?" she asked.

His mouth felt dry, and the space in his chest where only a fraction of his soul now lived was warm, pulsing so fast that he imagined it was the feeling humans had when their hearts beat erratically.

"I believe you and I share a soul." There, he'd said it again. It was as if the words wanted to be set free.

She blinked a few more times. "I believe I need tea. Would you join me in the drawing room?"

He followed as she turned, going down those nearly fatal stairs. It was a reminder of humans' frailty and fleeting existence on Earth.

Dina had convinced him to go in, saying Sanura would be easier to trap if one of them were already in the home. The other would guard from the outside. It was a bit of trickery, he knew, but he'd agreed, some part of him unable to say no.

When he'd touched her, his soul had leapt as if the universe had ground to a screeching halt. In his arms, encased in the most exquisite package, he'd held the missing half of his soul.

Now, he was overwhelmed with the urge to possess her. To protect her, even if she *had* stabbed him.

He sat, faintly aware of the way sitting on his wings always made him feel trapped. But it was a minor annoyance when her soul pulsed in time with his own, seeming to glow in her chest, and her pink lips slid apart, short panting breaths puffing between them as she watched him.

She sat in the chair across from him. Stood. "I'm sorry. Tea. How do you take it?"

Tea? She was asking about tea when thousands of years of suffering could be put right at long last?

"Tea?" he asked.

"Yes. Sugar?" She left the room; the pull at his chest was akin to stretching skin further than it wanted to go.

She stopped in the hall, rubbing her chest. "I... I'm quite unwell, actually," she called.

He stood, an irrational edge of panic riding his steps as he moved to her. He stopped beside her, and his soul calmed.

She leaned into the wall, looking up to meet his eyes. They were unfocused and coupled with her racing heart, he could only surmise she was in shock. Could he blame her?

"It's the strangest thing, but I am much recovered."

He nodded and held out a hand, his soul begging to be reunited by their touch once more.

She took it and gasped. "What was that?" She flinched away from him, pulling her hand free from his.

"It's the bond," he said, wondering again why he was talking to her as if she would understand any of what he was saying. But the words continued pouring from his mouth whenever she asked him about their connection.

Tentatively, she held a hand out again, pressing it to his cheek.

Every nerve in his body flared to life at her touch, his whole being straining to be closer. It was absurd. He didn't even know her name.

"Adalaide," she breathed.

So she could hear his thoughts as he could hers. Fascinating.

"Adalaide." He tested the name, tasting its sweetness on his tongue. *Adalaide and Gabriel.*

She smiled, her hand warm against his cheek as she let it rest there. "Gabriel. I like it."

He started back, breaking their touch. She was distracting him from his mission.

"There is a creature—a witch—who wants to kill you. I've come to keep you safe."

Adalaide dropped her hand to her side. "The woman from last night." She didn't say it as a question, and this new bond had her thoughts overriding her words in his mind. *What is he? What am I? Soulmates? Can that be true?*

She was far more concerned with him than the witch who was undoubtedly on her way to kill her. That was dangerous.

"You've warded the outside, but we should do more inside to keep you safe." Gabriel pushed off the wall, went back to the foyer, and spread his arms.

Such broad shoulders.

His mouth inched up at the corners, but he shook the thought away. She was destined to want him, to want to be near him. It was his soul longing to be reunited, nothing more.

He let out a long breath as he spread his fingers wide, casting a shield over the entry space. Finding minuscule bits of dust and debris, he wove them into the corners of the air shield, knitting them between splinters and frayed edges of wood along the floor to hold the shield in place, then did the same along the ceiling, stretching it tight.

He went to the back of her house, doing the same across the back door and windows, before moving to the second and third floors, securing each of the windows in a similar fashion. When every entry point was secure, he returned to the sitting room, finding Adalaide seated, scribbling furiously in her journal. The knife had found its way downstairs, he noticed.

He hadn't felt her leave; unlike the first time, when she had left to get tea, the bond seemed to accept they weren't parting from one another as he worked his way through the house.

Or perhaps she had already rejected him. Just the thought of her rejection sent a jolt of fear through him. It would be harder than he anticipated to leave when they'd finally rid the Earth of Sanura. Perhaps if she were finally gone, he wouldn't need to...

He cut the thought short, burying it deep. Thoughts like those were the sort that fed hope. Hope was a thing he had no use for. A stabbing pain shot through him, reminiscent of the day his soul had been wrenched in two. He dropped to his knees, gasping.

Adalaide looked up and shot to her feet, coming to his side. "Are you well?"

Her nearness soothed some of the ache tearing through him. "Tea," he wheezed.

She left quickly, and every step she took sent another stabbing pain through him. The bond recognized what he was doing. What *was* he doing? It was hard to think around the ache.

Then, she was back, holding a cup out to him. The pain receded, and when his fingers brushed hers, cool relief swept through him. He took a shaky breath, got slowly to his feet, and set the cup on a hall table.

"I have questions, Mr...," Adalaide said, pressing a hand to her hip.

He winced at the tone in her voice and at the slew of questions darting through her mind. She had a lot of them. "Seraphim do not have last names."

"Very well, I shall call you Gabriel if it's acceptable."

She watched him expectantly, tapping her foot. He was half a foot taller, but she managed to peer down her nose at him and damn if he didn't like it. Sitting, he shrugged his shoulders, attempting to shake off the tightness where his wingblades bent at odd angles.

"Gabriel, I wish you wouldn't sit on your wings. It's as unbearable for me as it is for you."

He started at that, releasing his hold on his illusion and freeing his wings to rest over the back of the couch. He let out the smallest sigh, stretching wing muscles behind his back.

Adalaide's mouth tightened, but it wasn't fear pinching those pink lips. "Now, I've made some notes on how you use your magic, and it's quite different from the way I use mine, but I believe we are working with the same tools. If that's incorrect, please stop me." She arched a brow at him, but when he said nothing, she went on. "You said we're tethered to one another." She stumbled over the word tethered as if she weren't sure if the word fit.

In her mind, the words *connected, soulmates, soul bonded* ran across her consciousness, but she said none of them. She raised her brow further, but he hadn't heard a question, so he said nothing, rubbing absently at his chest and the phantom pain lingering there.

"There's a woman who seems to fear you. You recognized her. It seems I've unwittingly stumbled into some feud between your two kinds."

How the hell had she put that together so quickly?

Her lips quirked up at the corners. "Right. So you're here to protect me from her because of this *tether*?" She said *tether* again as if she still wasn't sure it was the word she wanted to use. "I can only conclude that whatever you are, I am as well."

"No."

She waited, but when he said no more, she said, "Am I not warranted an explanation?"

The space in his chest that longed to be made whole pulsed again, and she looked down, letting him know she felt it, too.

"We aren't the same, but we share one soul."

Adalaide scrunched her nose up, making a face. "You've said as much. How can we share one soul if we're not the same sort of creature?"

"You have seraph blood, but you're human too."

"Seraph? Angel blood? You're an angel?"

He nodded.

"*I'm* part angel?" Her tone was incredulous.

Why did he preen over the fact that her incredulity was at her own lineage and not his? He'd never questioned who or what he was; why should she? And why should he care if she did? Why did anything this woman thought matter to him? A dull ache started in his chest again. A reminder that his soul *did* care.

Her racing thoughts were stumbling over so many possibilities he was having trouble keeping up. It was his first glimpse into the mind of a human. Were they all this erratic and scattered?

"And the creature who wants me dead, is she a demon?"

"A witch."

Adalaide let out a small laugh. "I have met many witches in my lifetime. That woman was no witch."

Gabriel leaned back in his chair. The way she ran over the multitude of variations of a question before she settled on the one she would speak aloud was confounding. She meant: I can't feel Sanura's magic and, therefore, cannot conceive of a scenario in which his statement could be true. Yet, I can taste lies, and that was no lie. So, where does that leave me?

He answered the question she hadn't asked aloud.

"Your seraph blood has gifted you with elemental magic. Only Nephilim carry the gift of all four elements. Witches are a dilution of our line. Somewhere along the line, human blood polluted their magic enough that they no longer carry all four elements.

"Sanura, the witch who hunts you, is of the line of a fallen angel; as such, her gifts are different from ours. She has the gift of necromancy. When she died, with help from her analogous umbra—her soulmate—she resurrected herself so she could exact revenge on those who killed her: your ancestors.

"I have hunted her for more than three thousand years."

CHAPTER 12

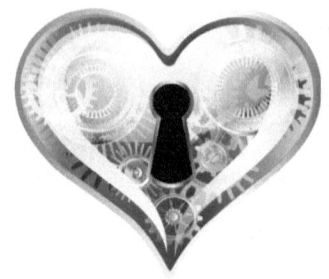

Adalaide

Adalaide sat back, slouching into her chair. She was glad for the hundredth time that night she'd chosen to forego her corset. If she weren't staring at massive wings draped over the back of her sofa as he spoke, and if she couldn't taste the truth in his words, she would have wondered what poison she had ingested.

But the moment he'd caught her on the stairs, something had changed inside her. Irreparably.

He'd said they were soulmates. Though she tasted the truth in that statement, she couldn't wrap her mind around it. In fact, she couldn't wrap her mind around *any* of it. An angel? Her? No, her soul was as dark as they came.

She held in a groan as she remembered the knife coated in his golden blood clattering to the floor. Had she actually stabbed an angel? If she weren't already destined for eternity in a fiery pit, certainly she was now. He didn't seem to be affected by the injury, though. Perhaps that counted for something.

A bout of exhaustion hit her and she yawned loudly, covering her mouth.

Gabriel sat forward. "What happened to your arm?"

She twisted her wrist, lips turning down at the dots of red soaking into her white sleeve. "It's nothing."

Gabriel slid to the edge of his seat, holding out his hand. "Let me see."

Adalaide tugged self-consciously at her cuff. "Pardon my saying so, but I hardly think it appropriate."

"Unbutton your sleeve and show me your injury."

A small thrill shot through her at his demanding tone. She bit her lip, glancing at the immense snow-white wings draped over her settee and slowly undid her cuff. Carefully, she folded back the sleeve, wincing at the angry line running down her arm. It had darkened at the seam, but the bright red under her skin was a bad sign. In the evening's excitement, she'd nearly forgotten the injury until now.

Gabriel sucked in a breath. "This shows signs of infection. Why didn't you tell me of your injury sooner?"

Adalaide huffed a laugh. "Am I meant to share the details of my life with you? I did not receive the missive."

His sable brows fell into a flat line as his eyes darkened. "I'm going to heal you. Remain still."

Adalaide's heartbeat picked up speed as he cupped his hands over her forearm and soft white light spilled from between his fingers. Her arm warmed beneath the healing glow before becoming blessedly cool as the infection dissipated.

When his hands lifted, her skin was smooth and creamy, all signs of her wound erased.

"Are you hurt anywhere else?"

Her cheeks flushed. But she shook her head.

"Do not lie to me."

The crimson staining her cheeks burned down her neck, and she rolled her bottom lip between her teeth. "I will manage."

"You will not. The necromancer's talons are poisoned. You'll only grow weaker. Show me."

She tasted the truth of his words and another thrill ran down her spine, this time laced with fear.

Squeezing her eyes shut, she found the buttons of her blouse and began undoing them one by one. When she'd unbuttoned enough to slip her blouse over one shoulder, she exposed the long red gash running up her biceps and trailing over her shoulder.

Warm fingers ran lightly over her skin, and she let out a breath, blinking open her eyes as the heat in her chest flared to life.

Swirling eyes of deepest charcoal skimmed over every inch of bare skin, and the fire in them made her squeeze her legs together.

Gabriel brushed a curl over her shoulder, exposing more flesh. A tremor ran through her and she leaned into his touch, giving in to the emotions warring within her.

Could this creature of unfathomable beauty truly be hers? Could she let herself believe for just a moment something *good* was hers? He cupped his hands over her second injury, warming her skin as he used his gift to heal her.

When his hands remained long after she was healed, she pressed closer, her eyes meeting his as she searched his face for any sign the words he'd said on the stairs were true. Were they meant to be together? Bound by some force of the universe?

Her face was inches from his, and she could taste the sweetness of his breath.

Shuddering, something in his eyes shifted, and he dropped his hands, leaning back. "You must be tired, Adalaide. I'll stay to keep watch."

She blinked as his rebuff washed over her. A cold stone settled in her stomach. He had rejected her. Of course he had. He was goodness and light and she was human and everything that entailed.

"Adalaide," he said gently.

How could she have ever imagined an angel—a perfect being—would want to be saddled with her? *Soulmates.* He'd said they were soulmates. But what did that matter when she would never be good enough for him?

Gabriel's brows drew together as he opened his mouth.

Suddenly, she knew hearing his next words would be more terrifying than anything she had encountered this night. She stood, pulling her shirt closed and turned, fleeing.

When she reached her room, she slammed her door and fell against it, sliding to the floor.

She closed her eyes, resting her forehead on her arms, and let the tears fall.

CHAPTER 13

Gabriel

When Adalaide's mind settled, the tears long dried and her racing thoughts calmed, he slouched against her bedroom door, listening to her soft breaths slowing until she was truly asleep.

He ran a hand over his face, wincing at the phantom pain in his chest.

It was nearly dawn, and there had been no further disturbances to the wards. He should go. Spending time with her was a mistake. They'd spent only one night together, but already, he couldn't imagine another moment without her.

Seeing those injuries inflicted by Sanura had made the feral beast inside him wild for vengeance. When he found the necromancer, he would break her.

He stood, backing away from the thin bit of wood separating him from the other half of his soul. His mind ran over her thoughts again. Her pain. She hadn't understood his actions. But her fragile human mind couldn't comprehend what it would mean for her. To accept the bond between them. Give in to the feelings pressing both of them to act.

The clock rang the sixth hour, signaling dawn's approach.

He stepped away from her door, squaring his shoulders. She didn't deserve that sort of half-life. And he wouldn't force it upon her.

Gabriel hit the ground, clutching his chest, and Dina appeared on the sidewalk beside him, sliding an arm under his.

"Get your illusion up," she hissed, glancing up and down the street.

He sucked in a scorching breath around the pain spearing through him and tried to focus on forcing his wings into a tailored coat. They glimmered, but he couldn't hold the illusion when the Earth rocked beneath his feet and the world threatened to tilt on its axis.

"Help me," he choked out.

Dina looked around the rapidly lightening streets before transforming and wrapping her arms around him. They landed just inside the gates of Alaxia and Gabriel took his first real breath since *she'd* opened the door last night.

That dull, hollow feeling was back, and he felt it more keenly now. The pain was gone, but the empty ache was nearly worse. To be severed from her by planes of existence was a torture all its own. He envied her that she couldn't feel what he did. Didn't know what the promise of a soul reunited felt like.

He passed under the arches of his room, sliding into his favorite golden chair and staring into his fireplace's crackling blue embers. His gaze grew unfocused as he thought back on the night. He'd been unable to stop himself from sharing the truth of their bond. He would not have lied; to do so was a sin unforgivable, especially to one's analogous umbra, but he'd never been burdened with an inability to hold his tongue.

With her, words spilled from his lips, anxious to be set loose upon the world. Was it like this for the others? *I could ask Dina.* He dismissed the thought as quickly as it came. Dina would counsel him to reunite their souls. As would all his brethren.

Perhaps in this moment, only the Fallen could begin to understand the fear that plagued him. He shook the thought from his mind. The Fallen had chosen to bond. Tethering himself to the creature whose magic was an abomination against nature.

Tethering. The word had sounded wrong when Adalaide used it. But perhaps it had been more right than she knew.

She would come to regret eternity with him.

Perhaps he should let her die at the hands of Sanura and rid them both of this unnecessary suffering. She could enter the gates of Alaxia freely and exist as the humans did for eternity, rather than the senseless half-life the Nephilim were forced to endure while their mates worked tirelessly for the humans.

But for the first time, he understood something he had not before. Though Aaron, and the Nephilim like him, felt intense longing when their other half was on the mortal plane, that excruciating ache was severed the moment they crossed over.

As whole soulmates, were they unburdened by the emptiness he felt?

Was it hope that was threatening to blossom once more inside him? He tamped it down, stuffing it deep into the recesses of his mind where all feelings better left unexamined lived.

"We must go back."

Dina's words cut into his thoughts, breaking him free from the dark place his mind had been headed. Sometimes, he wondered if she could read his thoughts by the way she timed her distractions.

He glanced up at his sister. "She will be safe for the day."

"What happened last night?"

He slumped back in his chair, staring deeper into the fireplace. "Not today, Dina."

Dina moved to stand in front of him, blocking his view of crackling blue flames. "She is your analogous umbra. I know she is. Why did we leave? Why are you suffering when you can be together?"

He waved a hand, sending her aside with a bit of air magic, and stared darkly into the flames. He would not have *this* fight today.

Dina moved again and pressed her nose into his face. He leaned back, giving her space, but she moved closer. This close, he could see the myriad of colors swirling beneath white brows drawn low.

"There is no path but this one. Why delay the inevitable?"

Gabriel growled, warning her to back up.

She ignored the warning, searching his face. "Why are you so determined to martyr yourself? Do you not deserve the same happiness as the rest of us?"

Gabriel's temper flared. He sat up straighter, stretching his wings wide in a show of dominance.

Dina backed up, showing deference to his broader wingspan.

Only one had outranked him. And his wings were gone now.

He stood. "I did not choose this punishment. I did not succumb to the temptation of mortal flesh, and yet I have suffered the most." He strode away, stopping at the bookshelf in the corner of his room. "Why, after so many millennia, am I finally shown this mercy? Perhaps it is no mercy at all but simply another punishment. Of all the Nephilim born over the centuries, why now? Why this one?"

"It does not feel like punishment to me, brother." Dina's words were soft.

For a moment, he thought she might give up this argument.

Instead, she said, "If she dies, you may never reunite your soul. Is it truly what you wish?"

He didn't answer. He couldn't. The lie poised to fall from his lips would mark him eternally in shame. But what did it matter if he wanted it? She did not deserve that fate. Better for them both to go on as if their paths had never crossed.

When it was clear he wouldn't answer, Dina shook her head. "I will protect her for as long as I can, brother, but if you don't unite with her before she dies, you will live like this until the end."

She left the room.

Gabriel paced, bare feet slapping against marble as he strode back and forth, wishing he could shut it off for a while—close his eyes as the humans did and go to sleep.

He could, of course, place his body in a form of stasis. Something rarely done, but for those tempted by desire, loss or longing, there was an option. It was meant to stave off a fall. Meant to ensure seraphim had another choice, one that didn't end in darkness and the absence of their Father's love.

He brushed the thought aside, resuming pacing. He needed a mission—something to take his mind from the woman and thoughts of what could be. Marching out of his room, he stopped at the arched door frame of Chamuel's room and knocked. A golden-haired man rose, draping himself against an arch.

"Gabriel, you look divine as always."

Gabriel raised a brow, peering around Pierre. "Is Chamuel here?"

Pierre turned to look behind him and seemed just as surprised as Gabriel to find he was alone. He shrugged. "It appears he is not."

Gabriel scowled, backing out of the doorway and stopping in front of Michael's door. "Michael?"

The angel looked up from his easel, giving him a bored smile. "I'm not interested in going on one of your missions to save the humans, *Gabriel*."

"I had hoped to join you on one of yours," he said, realizing the futility of asking Michael for anything as the words left his mouth.

Michael sighed. "I have no mission at present."

Of course he didn't. His time on Earth had long passed, and in his glory, he had been awarded a reprieve from further tasks.

The next several rooms were empty; most of his siblings were likely on the mortal plane. There were so many wars, famines, and political intrigues of late; it was a wonder he hadn't been called to some greater purpose. But he had been tasked with wiping nasdaqu-ush from the Earth at the dawn of their creation, and as he'd yet to succeed in fulfilling that task, it remained his only assignment.

When he reached Uriel's room, he knocked at the edge of a marble arch and waited as the pair drifted to the door, hands clasped. Something terrifyingly close to jealousy stirred in Gabriel. He shoved it down, forcing a bland smile onto his face.

"Uriel, I hoped to unburden you for a time. I am in search of a mission. Shall I take yours until you've settled into your new life?"

Uriel grinned sheepishly, giving his full attention to Henry. "Raphael has taken my mission," he said.

Gabriel ground his teeth. "Very well." He turned around, not waiting to hear more from the couple whose newly radiant haloes were jarring in their intensity.

After several more failed attempts, he found himself standing at the top of a great marble staircase. Below, hills sloped into an expansive distance. Dotted between the greenery were glowing orbs of light. They speckled the landscape, appearing as millions of tiny stars winking lazily among fields upon fields of green.

He wasn't sure why he'd come to the humans' domain. He rarely did, having so little interest in them. Today, something had called him, beckoning him to witness. This was where Adalaide would go when she died. Her soul would travel through the pearly gates and find its place among the others, drifting below. If...

He didn't finish the thought.

Seraphim couldn't communicate with the souls of humans, couldn't truly say whether they preferred this state of being to their human one, but it was where they would remain until the battle at the end of times reclaimed the Earth for Alaxia or failed.

They would remain in spirit form until they were ushered into a new era where planes collided, becoming one, and all their souls found solace in the new bodies their Father would create for them. When evil, death, and suffering were wiped from that plane, human souls would be given utopia.

But what if seraphim weren't welcome in that new paradise? Surely, their Naphil would stay with them. It was just another reminder that tethering her soul to his would mean suffering whatever fate awaited him and his brethren.

With new resolve, he marched toward the hall of chambers.

"I've been looking for you," Dina said, racing to his side.

Gabriel continued on his path, now more determined to leave Adalaide to whatever fate would release her from his grasp.

"I've seen Sanura. She's in Egypt, creating more of her creatures. She is building an army. I killed several, but I need you."

It was perfect. Just what he needed to distract him from *her*. "Let's go," he said, pulling out his sword.

They landed atop a stone and clay building as Gabriel ran a finger down the sword, setting it alight. A sandstorm whipped around them, obscuring their view and making it impossible for the humans to see them in solid form.

Screams rang out as creatures, too fast for the humans to escape, darted between buildings, wreaking havoc. A child dropped her blanket and turned in the whipping sand to grab it. A creature with glowing yellow eyes snatched the child by the hand, dragging her into the dark.

Gabriel darted into the alley, bathing it in blue flame as he swung for the creature, slicing its head cleanly from its body. The child stared, round-eyed, as the nasdaqu-ush toppled to the ground. Gabriel laid both hands on the creature, letting the wind carry its remains away.

One large round tear slid down the child's cheek as she backed into the corner, bumping into stacks of hay.

Gabriel held out a hand to the child, who cried out, pressing hard against the hay at her back. "I won't hurt you," he said in her language.

She blinked, peering past him to the wings stretched out to shield her from the cyclone of dirt and debris tearing through her village. Her tears dried, and she held out a small hand, wrapping dirty fingers around his much larger ones.

They moved through the storm, and he asked her to point out her home. It was little more than a shack, but the windows were boarded tightly, and he set her down in front of the door, waiting until she pushed it open before lifting off the ground and landing once more atop a building.

Nasdaqu-ush rarely attacked such small towns, but with all their men fighting the Ottoman Empire at the border, they were unprotected and easy targets.

The wind died, taking with it the immediate danger.

Gabriel leaned against a stone wall, gazing at the aftermath of their terror. In moments, his thoughts drifted to the night before, remembering the way he'd brushed her dark curls aside, fingers trailing lightly over Adalaide's fair skin as he traced the line of freckles disappearing beneath her shirt.

Dina landed beside him, shaking him from his thoughts. She gave him a knowing look, and he frowned as an ache settled in his chest. Even a battle with the nasdaqu-ush hadn't been enough to distract him from thoughts of *her*. He was in trouble.

CHAPTER 14

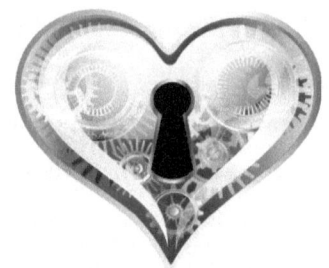

Adalaide

It had been three days since Gabriel knocked on her door, and Adalaide was beginning to wonder if the whole incident had been a dream. Her wards were real enough, though, and every time she ran a hand over the smooth skin along her forearm, she remembered his fingers skating lightly over her flesh.

But like the red-haired woman, he had not returned.

If he weren't just a hallucination, then he, like her father, had not found her worthy of him. She was too different, too strong for a woman, too curious. What did their supposed soul bond mean if even that was not enough to bring him back? And for a creature of Godly import, she was certainly unfit. Her eyes stung at the memory of his rejection.

She swiped at her tears, bending to pretend to admire a pair of jade earrings as a couple passed. When they moved on, she straightened, sniffling softly and steeling herself. No sense crying over a man who may never return. Straightening her shoulders, she pasted a demure smile across her face and nodded to another couple as they approached.

Adalaide set her shopping bags down at the breakfast table and began unpinning her bonnet. She continued working until all her curls were unbound, letting them fall down her back in loose waves. Sighing, she reached for a bottle of port and gave up counting as she let the glass fill nearly to the rim.

After a long day of snubs and snide looks on the promenade, followed by unnecessary shopping to ease her spirits, she wanted nothing more than to down a glass of port, unlace her stays, and breathe.

It wasn't yet dark, but it would take some time to erect the wards for the evening. Something told her the woman with red hair who had come to kill her would be back soon.

A knock at the door sent her heart into her throat. She stood, dumping her glass into the sink.

Was *he* back?

The knock came again and she pinched her cheeks, pulling her stays to tighten them as she hurried to the door. "Coming!" she called.

She flung the door open and froze as a woman dressed head to toe in white bowed slightly. "Good evening, Miss Graves. May I call at this late hour?"

Adalaide opened her mouth, but the woman breezed past, not waiting for her reply.

She closed the door, turning to face her guest. "Good evening. May I offer you some refreshments or tea?"

The woman tsked, looking Adalaide up and down. "Yes. I see it clearly."

Adalaide's mind stumbled over the words, wondering at their meaning. But humidity hung heavily in the air, and the unnatural breeze ruffling her hair told her at once that this was a witch with powerful magic. Her guard was up in moments.

"It's quite late. Might we continue this discussion tomorrow? I would be happy to call if you would just leave your—"

"I'll cut to it," the woman said. "You're in danger, and as a member of my bloodline, I have an interest in protecting you."

Adalaide swallowed, processing her words. "I'm sorry, Miss…"

"I'm Jophiel. Some have called me by other names, but you may address me as such."

Adalaide swallowed. "Apologies, but did you say your *bloodline*?"

Jophiel waved a hand. "In good time. First, we must get your wards up." She glanced around the room, seeing something Adalaide could not. "I see you haven't begun work tonight. I'll assist, and we will speak afterward."

Adalaide wanted to argue, to ask this strange witch to leave, but the breeze tickling her skin spoke of trust and honesty; she felt at once a deep sense of faith and calm.

Adalaide nodded, and she watched as Jophiel began setting wards around the inside of her house. It was different from the way Gabriel had done it; she wondered why she was comparing them. Where Gabriel leaned heavily on his air magic, Jophiel's inclination was to use fire magic first.

Adalaide's gift rose to the surface, humming under her skin. It begged to be united with its twin, but she tugged hard at the ember in her chest, banking the magic simmering just out of reach. One thought, one word, and it would ignite, but she let the witch do her work, watching in wonder at the way she used kinetic energy to force it into being instead of pulling it from her own internal spark.

It was a trick she longed to master, marveling at the possibilities of using a gift that did not draw from her own strength.

"There," Jophiel said when the house was encapsulated in an invisible force-field of kinetic energy, a bomb prepared to detonate at the first sign of intrusion.

Jophiel truly was a master of her craft.

"Would you care to sit?" Adalaide asked, gesturing toward the sitting room.

Jophiel inclined her head and they moved into the room, each sitting opposite one another.

Adalaide bit her lip, unsure what to do or say next. She entertained so infrequently; certainly, her guests were never strangers who had just performed magic and declared themselves to be of her bloodline. She opened her mouth. Closed it, glancing at the portrait of a long-dead relative over Jophiel's head.

"I want to teach you how to hone your gifts," Jophiel said after an uncomfortably long silence.

Adalaide nodded. "I would be grateful."

Jophiel dipped her chin, and again, they sat in silence, neither making a move.

"Also," Jophiel said after another long pause, "I wish to impart that Gabriel is quite well."

Butterflies erupted in Adalaide's stomach at the sound of his name. "You are acquainted with Gabriel?"

"Yes, dear. He is my brother."

CHAPTER 15

Gabriel

Gabriel's sword swung in a wide arc, taking off three heads, one after another. He spun, running the flaming blade through another creature, and it dissolved under his touch. Three raced for him, and he spread his blue-hued fingers wide, shooting bolts of flame at all three. They dropped silently. He turned, surveying the space.

It was pitch dark, the tents of sleeping soldiers undisturbed; he could only hope he'd killed them all.

The nasdaqu-ush were working with the Ottomans. Had they succeeded this night, they would have wiped out the Egyptian army and left the victory—quite decisively—to the Ottomans come morning.

Running a finger over his blade, he moved silently, laying both hands on each of the slain creatures, dissolving them. When they had all been dispensed, he stopped at the edge of camp, listening for the demons he knew would come.

Where there was a battle, there were always demons. They were drawn to it; like a sweet aphrodisiac, they could not stay away. They would whisper deceit and fear in the minds of the sleeping soldiers.

There, in the distance, sliding silently in and out of tents, he spied a dark, wispy creature. It looked up, sensing him, its red eyes slanted in the dark. It moved quickly, slipping into the nearest tent.

Gabriel stopped just outside the tent and dissolved into dust, letting the wind carry him inside. In the tent, he floated around the demon, watching as he leaned in and whispered in a sleeping man's ear. The man tossed and turned.

The demon smiled, seeming to sense Gabriel's presence.

Much as he would like to interfere, the demon was within his rights to test the man. So long as he did not inhabit him, Gabriel could do nothing but watch.

The demon's red eyes swirled with devious intent, and he rose, gliding through one tent flap and into the next.

Gabriel followed, watching with growing contempt as the demon planted fear and doubt in the next man's heart. The man would not die tonight at the hand of a nasdaqu-ush, but he would surely die tomorrow, for nothing killed more swiftly than crippling fear and doubt.

Gabriel solidified outside the next tent, leaving the demon to his work.

Would that he could save these humans, but the treaty, signed into being thousands of years ago, forbade him from interfering —at the cost of his own divine immortality.

He stopped at the edge of camp, sucking in a breath when he saw more than a dozen demons slipping between tents. They would undoubtedly turn the tide of the battle and perhaps the war, but he was helpless to intercede.

His soul pulsed, warming, tearing him from his thoughts. Adalaide was using her magic—*their* magic. And a great deal of it.

Was Sanura back? Was she even now fighting her and losing?

The ember at his chest tugged at him, begging him to return, to stand at her side. But he had agreed to swap missions with Dina, and if he left now, he would be going back on his word. In truth, he was afraid. Perhaps it was the influence of the demons wearing on him, but he could admit that he was scared to return to her, see her.

Dina was there. She would keep her offspring safe.

Another tug at the bond sent searing heat through his veins. His very being raged against his decision to leave her to whatever fate awaited.

It was torture. It was nothing less than he deserved.

Something sharp and painful shot through him, and he sank to his knees. Was it the bond rejecting his decision? Was it Adalaide dying? He couldn't tell. Couldn't breathe.

If she were dying, the pain would surely end soon. He could go back to the half-existence he was living, and she would ascend to Alaxia, to the fields humans were encapsulated in until the end.

A great burning pain cut his breath in two, making him curl into himself. It was agony such as he had never known. Even when his soul had been cleaved in two, it was a moment, a flash. This was unending torment.

She was dying. He wasn't there to save her. A scream tore from his throat, and he closed his eyes, blinking out of existence, back to Alaxia, where the pain dulled the moment his feet touched marble.

He sat, curled in on himself, breathing raggedly. Even across planes, a mild ache radiated through his being. It raged against his complacency, his acceptance of her fate.

She was his; he was hers. This was a violation of every natural law.

The reprieve he'd come to Alaxia for only worsened the void in his chest. Where pain had been all-consuming, he'd forgotten the vacuous state of the space his soul once occupied. Now, he was acutely aware of nothing else.

It was a hole so dark it would consume him.

A warm hand landed on his head, wrenching him out of his misery and bringing him back to the present. He looked up, gasping as he met Aniel's sad stare. Aniel, who had not spoken in more than a thousand years.

Not since the death of his analogous umbra.

A cry of desolation left his lips as Aniel held out his hands. He clasped arms with his brother, who pulled him up.

They stood eye to eye, an unspoken bond forming between them. Aniel shook his head and beckoned for Gabriel to follow.

They moved silently down the long hall of chambers inside the gilded palace, making their way to a room at the end.

They stopped in front of a gleaming fountain. Gabriel understood. Aniel hadn't made that choice when his other half died before she could accept him. But he was offering it to Gabriel. Drink from the chalice and find the closest thing to peace for a seraph.

It was the only way to escape their eternity—the only way to be free of the pain.

Aniel nodded, squeezing Gabriel's arm. He would be there. He would bear witness. And when Gabriel's still form was laid beside the others who had chosen this fate, he would rest. He would be free of the unending suffering that would plague him at knowing how close he had come to reuniting with his soul's other half, only to have it ripped from him.

He swallowed, meeting Aniel's eyes again. They swirled, dark, like his, with such misery he felt all at once they would be kindred in this no matter what end.

"Why didn't you do it?" he asked into the silence.

Aniel looked at the chalice, now cupped in Gabriel's tense fingers, and backed up. He touched Gabriel's arm lightly and moved to the open archway overlooking green fields.

Gabriel had never realized this room was so near the human fields. Not that he'd come to this room often. Perhaps twice in his long existence. Once for Hutriel and again with Baraqiel.

He looked out at the buzzing glow of so many souls, then back to Aniel. "You're waiting for her."

Aniel dropped his gaze to the floor.

Long moments passed where Gabriel considered what it must be like to spend eternity waiting for a soul who had died before she had the chance to bond with him. What if, at the end of it all, she didn't choose him?

An echo of the pain he felt on the mortal plane shot through him. Here in Alaxia, pain, sickness, and death did not occur. But emotions such as anger and sadness existed across all planes, and he was beginning to learn they could be worse than anything physical.

Aniel finally met his stare and nodded once.

So much was imparted in that one gesture. It was the hope that bloomed eternal against all odds. The hope that even in an uncertain existence, where nothing was guaranteed, and pain and suffering were sure to be long bedfellows, Aniel chose to believe all would be set right in the end.

Gabriel set the chalice down and squeezed Aniel's arm. "Thank you, brother."

CHAPTER 16

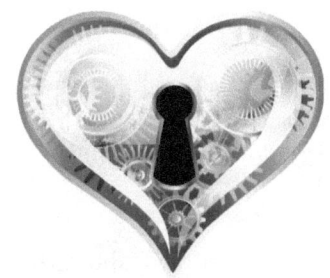

Adalaide

Adalaide took shallow breaths, sucking in around the brick settling atop her lungs.

"Be still," Jophiel said, placing both hands over the wound piercing her chest.

Light began to glow under Jophiel's cupped fingers, and she spoke softly. As she did, Adalaide took deeper and deeper breaths, inhaling with relief. What might have surely been a fatal wound was stitching itself together quickly, and the poison lingering in her chest was rapidly dissolving into nothing.

When Jophiel had finished, Adalaide sat up, touching the tender flesh below her breast. She could feel a bit of scar tissue settling under her ribcage, but her lungs were blessedly free of fluid.

"Thank you," she panted, taking in another deep breath.

Jophiel patted her arm. "Next time, we will be better prepared."

Adalaide inhaled sharply. She wasn't sure how many more of these kinds of attacks she could withstand. Was this to be her life now? Fighting demons and nasdaqu-ush, as Jophiel had called them, every other night?

She was worn thin.

In less than a fortnight of Jophiel's tutelage, she'd learned to expand her gifts tremendously, pulling from nature rather than expending her own lifeforce, but even with all her abilities, demons and nasdaqu-ush—when they came by the dozen—were a daunting task.

She'd taken to sleeping all day and fighting or training all night, and already, her muscles felt more toned.

Her raging fire was more controlled, and she'd learned to harness water in new and interesting ways.

Despite it all, something pulled at her chest, an ache that would not subside, and no matter how she filled her nights, she thought of the tall, handsome stranger who had darkened her door only once, never to return.

Jophiel glanced out the window at the rapidly swelling orb peeking over the horizon and back to Adalaide. "Rest for the day. I will be back before nightfall."

Adalaide nodded, wincing as she stared down at her destroyed waistcoat and corset. "Help me remove these before you go?"

Jophiel nodded, helping her slip out of her overcoats and gingerly removing her corset and undergarments until Adalaide was blessedly nude. Jophiel turned away, unbothered by her nudity, and moved to the door. "Sleep, Adalaide. You will need it."

Adalaide stretched out on her bed, letting soft yellow streaks paint her skin as she reveled in the warmth of the morning sun. It relaxed some of the tension.

Bits of dust, caught in the light, swirled through her fingers as she raised them, twisting until they formed an infinity loop in the air above her.

A draft from the window wafted through the room, sending goosebumps across her skin, and she watched as her loop dissipated, flecks of dust dropping lazily to her bare skin. They fell in a strange pattern, settling over her new scar as if to inspect the damage.

She laughed, watching them scatter as she ran a finger down her smooth stomach, sending the particles of sparkling dust into the air once more.

Smiling, she rolled over, wrapping herself in the blankets and closed her eyes. For just a moment, she imagined her angel was in the room with her, his arms wrapped around her as she drifted off to sleep.

CHAPTER 17

Gabriel

Gabriel waited till her breathing slowed and she was truly asleep before he solid-ified in her room.

Where a human woman's nakedness would have chased him away before, he had slipped into her room only to be struck speechless by the exquisiteness of her lithe body.

Caught in her magical pull for just a moment, he'd reveled in the sensation of her fingers lovingly caressing his insubstantial form as she wove the particles of dust that made him between her fingers before allowing him to settle on her new scar.

It was healed. Some part of his being settled into a deep calm seeing her made right by Dina's hand. For that, he would be infinitely grateful.

When she stirred his being into the air, giving him a more breathtaking view of her perfect form, it was all he could do to stop himself from forming and claiming her then and there.

But moments after their intimate dance, she had rolled into her blankets, a look of absolute contentment on her serene face, and some broken part of his soul had mended just a little.

How could this perfect creature have been made just for him?

In the darkest parts of his mind, he balked at the idea that it could ever end well. He was undeserving. If he sought to capture this bit of happiness for himself, the universe would conspire to take it from him.

Adalaide mumbled something, turning onto her side. He opened his mind, letting her jumbled, incoherent dream thoughts in.

He started. Though they had only met once, her thoughts were consumed with images of him. He was smiling, then frowning. He ran a finger up her arm as heat blazed in his gaze. He was on his knees, agony painted across his face, and she reached out to him tentatively as she laid a hand on his arm. Everything inside her bloomed, lighting up. The dark corners of her mind were illuminated, casting all her fears into harsh clarity.

She backed up, closing her eyes as all her dark emotions crowded out of the shadows. Suddenly, the dream took a turn; Adalaide was standing in the kitchen holding up both arms. A woman was behind her, and a man wielding fire stood in front of them.

"You're nothing. Who do you think made you? I can destroy you just as easily."

The man lifted his hands in the air, waving them theatrically, and red flames danced along his fingers. Black tinted the edges of his flame's red glow, speaking of the dark magic corrupting him from within.

Even inside her dream, Gabriel could feel Adalaide waver. She didn't want to hurt her father. She was stronger than him, but she knew he would never stop if she let him live.

The woman behind her, her mother, let out a small cry. "He's your father, Adalaide. Don't hurt him."

Gabriel knew this wasn't what she'd really said. It was Adalaide's guilt speaking. The woman in her mind blamed Adalaide for what came next.

The man, her father, sent a streak of fire running across the counter. It wasn't meant to kill but to distract. He wasn't planning to do it himself.

He was waiting.

A dark figure darted into the room. *Astaroth.* Gabriel knew him well. One of the Fallen's lieutenants, trusted to carry out many of his very dark deeds. That he was here could mean only one thing: the Fallen was personally invested in the outcome. Astaroth would not have been sent for anything less.

Pieces clicked into place in Gabriel's mind. How had he not seen it sooner? Sanura wasn't acting alone. Her mate was pulling strings of his own to ensure she got her revenge. How had none of them seen this was the reason she'd never failed?

With the help of her lover and his army of demons, along with her nas-daqu-ush, they were virtually unstoppable.

Adalaide's father shot a quick sequence of fireballs at her, two hitting her mother as she dodged. It was a distraction. Astaroth dived, sinking his teeth into her neck. She screamed, pressing two blue-tinged palms into his chest, and he released her, hissing.

The pair circled her, Astaroth moving behind while her father remained in her direct line of sight. He raised both hands, shooting ball after ball of flame at her. She threw up a shield blocking him, but while she was distracted, Astaroth dived for her mother, spearing her with poison-tipped claws.

Adalaide screamed, sinking to the floor beside her mother. In that same moment, something inside her detonated, a blue flame exploding through the room. Astaroth winked out of the room, leaving Adalaide's mother and father to be obliterated by the blow.

Gabriel pulled himself from her mind, shaking the emotions riding her dream from his head.

Adalaide tossed and turned, fighting her blankets until she was uncovered, the silhouette of her pale skin luminous in the soft light of the morning sun. Her nails dug into the comforter, tearing fabric, and soon, a light plume of feathers exploded into the space, hovering erratically.

Trapped in her nightmare dreamscape, they whirled madly above her.

She screamed.

Gabriel lurched forward, wrapping her in the blankets and settling onto the bed beside her, tucking her against his chest. She calmed, relaxing easily into his embrace. Something in his chest settled, too, soothing the ache that had not subsided since he'd felt her nearly die.

She sighed contentedly, and he let himself slip into her mind again.

In her dream, he was sitting across from her, crowded uncomfortably into a small space he didn't recognize. His wings scraped the ceiling, and the chair he was crammed into was made of a strange white material.

She, too, was dressed strangely, in men's pants like none he'd seen before. Her hair was short and cut above the neck, and there was a hardness to her features that this version of her did not possess.

The scene changed, and she was in a hall lined with windows. Lifting one hand, she watched in fascination as dust swirled between her fingers. He knew instinctively he was there. He was that dust, straining to be near her.

She looked so different. Had he not seen this dream, knowing it for what it was, he would not have known it was her. But this was a vision. She was dreaming of a future he couldn't imagine. A future where she had not aged, though the world around her was transformed.

CHAPTER 18

Adalaide

Adalaide stretched, feeling the pull of new scar tissue below her ribcage, confirming at least some of last night had not been a dream. She ran a hand over the empty space beside her where she'd dreamed Gabriel had lain.

She glanced out the window and sat up. The last vestiges of daylight crept quietly behind their veil, casting the world outside in that eerie time between day and night. She had slept the day away, and now she was left with very little time to ward the house before someone new came to kill her.

After the horrid night she'd had and the dream of her parents' deaths, she ought to be in one of her moods, but she found there was a lightness in her chest she couldn't explain. Perhaps it was the inkling which lived inside her, guiding her path, warning her when danger was near. It was telling her no foul thing would find her this night.

She slid out of bed, padding lightly to the boudoir in the corner of her room and pulled out a loose top that buttoned up the front and a pair of riding breeches. They were made for men, but they allowed her freer movement on the nights she would need to fight for her life, and those were becoming more and more frequent.

Dressing quickly, Adalaide rushed to the back hall, raising her arms to begin the work Jophiel had been teaching her. Her fire magic was strong, making it easy to follow, but her natural inclination was to use her air magic.

She stopped, biting her lip.

A strong air shield was woven against the wall. She tested it, pressing her own magic tentatively into it. The magic was absorbed, embracing hers as if in a warm hug.

"Gabriel?"

The ember at her chest pulsed, and she spun, sucking in a sharp breath.

He was there, arms folded over his chest, massive white wings splayed wide behind him. Her gaze trailed the length of him, finding him even more beautiful than she remembered. A nervous thrill ran through her. She'd thought he would never return when Jophiel came and came again each night.

His lips pressed into a thin line.

The ember in her heart warmed, charging in his presence, and thoughts began to slip into her mind.

Should leave. Should go. Dangerous. Perfect. Torture. Selfish.

His thoughts, some in contrast to one another and the last—nonsensical—made her heart sink. He didn't want to be there. With her. He was likely only there to ward her home because Jophiel had been called to some other task.

She was reminded again of the way they'd parted the last time they saw each other. The only other time they'd spent together. A sharp pain pierced her breast, leaving her gasping for air. She leaned into the wall.

Gabriel uncrossed his arms, his leg twitching as if to move. Toward her? Away? She wasn't sure; the fact that his thoughts had gone silent sent fresh pain through her chest.

"I'm not sure why you came," she managed through shallow breaths. "Jophiel has taught me all I need to ward my home from the creatures. There was no need to trouble yourself over me."

She didn't say she'd rather not see him if it only caused them both pain. She didn't say she wished he'd close the distance and press his lips to hers.

By the way his face changed, she didn't need to say anything aloud. Though he knew the trick for keeping his thoughts from her, she certainly did not know how to reciprocate.

He said nothing, watching her as thoughts continued to tumble through her mind. It was as if they were having some silent, one-sided conversation in the hall outside her room—the room where she'd been sleeping naked while he was warding her house.

Her cheeks flamed.

Had he come into her room? Seen her? It should have felt like a violation to consider it, but she found she really only wanted to know if her naked form appealed to him.

His lips quirked up at the corners. The devilish look on his face made a riot of butterflies erupt in her stomach. Perhaps she had misinterpreted his thoughts before. Some of them...

As quickly as it had arrived, the look was gone, and he crossed his arms once more.

"I beg your pardon. Were you going to say something or simply stand in my hallway staring at me all night?"

At that, he looked properly chastised, and she grinned.

"No."

She nearly rolled her eyes. "No, you weren't going to say anything, or no, you weren't intent on barricading my path?"

"You were injured. I came to see you had recovered."

Adalaide arched a brow, waiting for him to say more, to elaborate on his sudden concern for her welfare after leaving her in Jophiel's care for weeks. When he said nothing, she sighed.

"As you can see," she waved a hand down her body, "I'm quite well. You may return to your life as it were before we met."

He pursed his lips, looking her up and down, and she could have sworn he was on the verge of some revelation equally as devastating as the one he'd laid upon her the night he entered her home and declared himself her soulmate.

Instead, he dipped his head, giving her a shallow bow. "Very well. Good evening, Adalaide."

A strangled sob caught in her throat.

His wings vibrated, and he took one step toward her.

She held her breath.

He took another step, closing the distance between them, and lifted her hand to his lips, pressing a soft kiss against the bare skin of her knuckles.

Every nerve in her body sizzled, zeroing in on the place where his skin met hers. *My light in eternal darkness.* She heard the words as clearly as if he'd spoken them. His fingers tightened around hers, and he looked up, black pools dragging her into their depths.

She was frozen, unable to move, unable to speak.

He released her hand, shaking his head and dissolving into nothing.

She gasped, spinning in a circle, but he was gone. The ache in her chest throbbed in hollow longing. He had left her alone. Again.

CHAPTER 19

Gabriel

Gabriel landed just outside the arched frame of his room and stepped in.

He dropped heavily into the chair beside his hearth and released his first real breath since she'd stepped out into the hallway and called his name.

Why did his name on her tongue make him want to fall at her feet and beg for her to say it again? Why did the frantic tumble of her thoughts so enthrall him? But that brilliant mind of hers had settled heavily on their last encounter. On his rejection.

He'd understood in that moment that the pain felt since meeting her was his soul warning him of the treacherous fate awaiting him if he rejected her for good. And that *was* what he'd intended. The moment she'd considered rejecting him, she'd felt the same pain.

He would have to be the one to let her go. To spare her the suffering that came with it, he would keep his distance. The thought sent an echo of pain through him. He had been weak to go there. To see her.

He'd meant to ward her home, see she was safe, and leave, but he had lost track of time. Wrapped in his arms, she had soothed the sharp edges of all he'd suffered that week. Selfishly, he longed to cherish the feeling just a bit longer.

When she woke, he should have left, but he hadn't the strength. And when his name spilled from her lips, he was undone.

He'd had a fleeting moment of elation, forming a mad plan to convince her to bond. He would do it then and there, ensuring whatever outcome. She would join him in Alaxia when her mortal form expired, but after a night in her mind, reliving her worst moments, he knew how selfish it would be. She deserved to be at peace, to rest with her mother—and perhaps even her father—when she died.

Even now, he wrestled with his selfish desire to make her his.

A knock in his doorway brought him out of his dark thoughts.

"Brother, we mount an offensive within the hour and could use your aid," Chamuel said from just outside the door.

He turned, gazing past Chamuel to the group of seraphim gathered in the hall. They stood in various poses, all looking expectant. Chamuel had gathered quite a horde.

"To what purpose?"

"The conflict in Syria escalates. The demon populous is lost to their lust. They have begun inhabiting the humans. We must quell them."

Gabriel stood shaking off the emptiness in his chest. Vanquishing demons was just the distraction he needed to take his mind off *her*.

He had a fleeting thought that he ought to tell Dina he would be gone for an unforeseen amount of time but thought better of further interference in the girl's life. He strode for the door, following Chamuel and the others out.

He could do this for her. For her, he would leave and give her the chance to ascend and be with the humans she loved for a peaceful eternity, and when the end came and the humans were made whole, she would take her place among them.

He landed first, faster than his brothers and sisters, and drew Dina's sword, running a hand down steel. Around him, humans cried out, blades singing as they swung against one another. Blood flew, coating the earth.

Between them, dark, insubstantial forms glutted themselves on the death and despair permeating the land. Lost to their own insatiable desires, they joined in the fray, inhabiting bodies and killing with abandon.

Gabriel charged into the battle.

A human, wild-eyed and disjointed, ran for him, and he knew at once it was possessed. He dropped his sword, pressing both hands on either side of the man's head and pushed the demon out, calling his soul back.

The man slumped to the ground as a dark form slid from his nostrils and began to solidify before Gabriel. He'd been too late for this man. His soul had already departed the Earthly plane.

Tugging his sword out of the ground, he stabbed the demon before it had fully formed. It blinked out of existence as another demon coalesced behind it. The man had been inhabited by two of the foul beasts.

Gabriel killed it quickly and dived to the ground as two demons inhabiting humans lunged for him. They hovered half-in and half-out of the human bodies. Their poison-tipped barbs wouldn't have killed him, but the pain it caused was enough to have him ducking.

They turned, circling back for another attack. He sucked in a breath, blowing hard as they approached.

Caught in his gust of air, they flew back several feet. Both redoubled their efforts, diving again the moment he stopped blowing. He reached for them, but they dodged out of the way.

A sharp pain in his back had him whirling around, growling as he took off the head of a smaller demon. The human it had inhabited slumped to the ground, and he wrenched the demon's talon from his back only to be speared in the shoulder. Spinning, he swung his sword wide, catching one of his attackers through the middle and sending it back to Primoria. The second dived for him again, and he swung, slicing through its chest. It disappeared, and he stuck his sword in the ground, leaning into it.

The poison in his back was deep, and it spread quickly, numbing the area. He swiveled his gaze, searching for a brother or sister to heal him. With the amount of venom pumping through him, healing himself would be difficult.

Another demon charged toward him, and he lifted his sword with his left hand, swiping for it. It danced back, easily avoiding his strike. The numbness was spreading, making it difficult to wield the sword. Seeing his weakened state, the demon charged him once more, and he feinted left, swinging for its middle.

An iron grip caught his wrist, stopping the fatal blow.

"Brother. That one is not inhabiting a human." Gabriel blinked at Remiel and back to the demon floating on a phantom wind. The creature leered at him before dissolving into nothing.

Gabriel clapped Remiel on the back. "Thank you, brother. That was too close."

He cast another look over the dust-caked bloody crowd, wincing at the poison creeping through his veins.

"Come," Remiel said, leading the way off the battlefield.

When they reached a bare patch of ground, Remiel turned, pressing both hands into Gabriel's back. Gabriel sighed as the numbness receded, followed by stinging pain. It was doing nothing to stifle the stab of agony in his chest, but magic would not heal that ache.

Gabriel spread his wings, lifting off the ground and soared over the mass of writhing, bloodied bodies. It stretched on in every direction, reaching all the way to the treeline. Though not the most significant battle he'd ever witnessed, it was of large enough scale that casualties would be great no matter the outcome.

At night, while the humans butchered one another with their failed medical practices, sawing limbs and digging into flesh to pull out bits of metal, the real attack would begin.

He would need to be here—they all would—to stop the worst of it.

For one moment, he let himself consider what Adalaide might be facing tonight, then, spying Chamuel disappear beneath a pile of dark creatures, he dived, letting thoughts of her drift to the periphery of his mind as he landed and began swinging.

CHAPTER 20

Adalaide

It had been another fortnight. Some small part of her mind was counting. Fourteen days. The last time he'd come, it was fourteen days after the first.

But the night came and went, and he never showed. With no new attacks and nothing to occupy her time, she thought of *him*.

Jophiel came each night, showing her some new way to use her gift. On the fifteenth night, she waited by the door, and when there was a knock, she threw it wide.

Crimson lips stretched into a cruel smile, and bright yellow eyes glimmered in some unnatural light.

Adalaide slammed the door, her chest heaving as she slouched against it.

The witch was back. She was here to kill her, and Jophiel had not come.

Adalaide had set her own wards, following all the instructions Jophiel had taught her, and woven in a few of her own—ones she'd seen Gabriel create.

"How unkind," a voice said from the other side of the door. "It's impolite to close a door in your guest's face."

Gabriel, she thought. *Gabriel, please come.* But wishing for him was as useless as wishing for her mother and father to be alive. She could only hear his thoughts when he was near, if he let her, and she had a feeling it was the same for him. If she hoped to survive another attack from the creature outside, she would need to be strong. She would need to be clever.

"You're not welcome, and you're no guest of mine," she called through the door.

"Come, Adalaide. I will make it quick. I promise."

Adalaide's heart stuck in her throat, the thrum of its rhythm making her breath come in short gasps. The wards were meant to hold off the creatures who had hunted her these past eight years, but the woman outside was so much stronger than they had ever been.

She stepped away from the door, frantically tracing the shape of a five-pointed star in the air. She called on the words in her journal, written in her father's hand, some bit of dark magic meant to hold their victim in place.

They were charged by demon magic, but perhaps she was strong enough to make it work. She ran to the kitchen, pulling a knife from the drawer, cutting her finger, and returning to the foyer. She traced the star shape she'd made with her bloody finger and let out a small sigh of relief as the blood dissolved, accepted by the spell.

A loud bang against the door sent her stumbling back, but it held. It was due entirely to the magic and had nothing to do with the extra money she'd spent on a reinforced door—she was sure of that. A creature such as Sanura would not be deterred by wood and steel.

Another loud bang at the door had Adalaide backing up.

She didn't know how long the wards would hold, so she used the time to construct another two magical traps in the foyer. They would slow her down, at the very least.

When no sound had come in some time, she dared to peek through one of the windows beside the door. It was dark and quiet. Had Sanura given up for the night?

A crash and the sound of shattering glass on the second floor made Adalaide's heart race, and nausea roiled in her gut as the ward across her second-floor window failed and zapped some of her energy. Steadying herself, she ran for the sound, lighting both hands in blue flame as she reached the second-floor landing and halted.

Hovering before her were two dark, insubstantial creatures. The one to the right whipped her tail in agitation, reminding Adalaide of a cat. The one to the left appeared at ease, making Adalaide more anxious.

She lifted both hands, forming balls of fire in them. "Don't come any closer."

The one to the left eyed her blue flame warily, but the catlike one gave a feral scream and lunged forward.

She met the creature, pressing both hands into her face and shoved with all her might, closing her hands into fists as the demon dissolved.

She turned her attention to the second demon, lifting shaking arms.

The toll of maintaining the wards, creating new traps below, and casting fire was wearing on her fast. The demon's horned brow rose as he observed her.

A loud bang and a cracking sound at the door below drew her attention.

The demon dived for her, wrapping sharp talons around her throat. She gasped as the tips dug into her delicate flesh. Where they drew blood, her skin burned, and she let out a rasping cry.

She wrapped her fingers around his, trying to pry them from her throat as his dark skin popped and sizzled under her flaming touch.

He hissed, releasing her, and she staggered forward, sucking in lungfuls of air.

Her skin was swollen and raw; she touched her neck, feeling the wet warmth of her own blood as it ran down her throat.

Another thud against the door and a crack below.

The demon was hovering just out of reach, waiting for her next move, but the stinging skin at her throat made her vision blurry. Soon, she would be no match for him.

She splayed her fingers, creating balls of flame and tossed them at him. He dodged them easily and lunged for her again. This time, she was ready for him, and she pressed both hands against his face, forcing as much energy into the flame as she could. He dissolved into nothing, and she fell to her knees.

She wanted to curl up on the floor and cover her head until it was all over, but no one was coming to save her. She would have to be strong if she hoped to survive the night.

Hope. It was a word she rarely used. Hope was a thing for children. It was for those who were blind to the world's depravity and torment. She had faced a father who had wanted her dead and eight years of creatures like these. Some distant part of her mind asked if it wouldn't be easier to let them end her.

A soft breeze at the back of her neck spoke of more to come this night. She rose unsteadily to her feet. *Not tonight,* she told the demons coming for her.

The next thud from the first floor sounded ominous as the door groaned.

She leaned against the wall, sliding to the floor. Breathing was becoming a chore, and dark spots dotted her vision.

She pressed both hands to her neck, saying the spell for healing.

A jolt ran through her, zapping her energy, and she slid further down. She had used too much of her life force tonight, and yet, she could feel the wards around the house humming merrily. They took and took with no regard for their toll on her.

"Jophiel," she whispered.

Her vision darkened, and she was vaguely aware of the wind telling her a story of the night's end. Of *her* end. She blinked, and the world flashed white. She blinked again, and then it was moving by at a strange angle.

When Adalaide opened her eyes, she took a long, even breath, grateful for the air filling her lungs, and stared blearily around the brightly lit space. She was in her room, buried beneath a shredded comforter, and all around her, tufts of down floated lazily in the air. She attempted to sit up, but a throbbing at her temple sent her sinking back into the blankets.

"You're lucky to be alive," a voice thrummed like the strings of a harp being plucked to create fine music.

She scanned the room, searching for the owner of the voice.

Jophiel moved to the bed, standing over her. "Don't attempt to sit up, Ada."

"I'm thirsty," Adalaide croaked.

Jophiel nodded, leaving the room.

Alone with her thoughts, she scrambled to put the events of last night in order.

Jophiel returned with a cup of water and sat beside her on the bed.

Adalaide pushed herself up, resting her back against the headboard, and took the cup gratefully. She sipped, relishing the cool liquid against her sore throat. Although it was healed, it felt raw. It would be her constant reminder of her latest near-death encounter.

"Ada, may I be frank with you?" Jophiel said, startling her from her thoughts.

"Please," she said, clearing her throat.

"You're not strong enough to beat Sanura. She has innumerable creatures at her disposal, and she has the help of the Fallen. There is no outcome that ends in your favor."

Adalaide swallowed. "You're painting a grim picture."

"I don't mean to frighten you, but I can assure you there is a place for you when you die."

The idea of death sent a jolt of fear through Adalaide. All people died. It was inevitable. But to think of it now, at twenty-three, was devastating. She had thought she had time to become... something.

"To seek your place beside your seraphim kin, you must bond with your soulmate."

83

Adalaide let out a derisive laugh. "There's no chance of that."

Jophiel rose, looking troubled. "I will admit, he's struggling to come round to the idea, but it is an inevitable fate... unless you die first."

Adalaide watched Jophiel as she paced the room. She took another sip of water. "How am I to accomplish such a thing when he's opposed?"

Jophiel spun to face her. "You're not, then? You would have him?"

"I would." The words left Adalaide's mouth of their own accord, and she tasted their truth. She didn't know him. Nor he her, but if there was a way to tie herself to him inexorably, she was sure she would do it.

Jophiel nodded once. "We have little time. Sanura could be back at any moment, but I have a plan."

CHAPTER 21

Gabriel

Gabriel stumbled into the archway of his room, leaning against it. He was bone weary, and although the magic all seraphim possessed wiped them of dirt and grime, he had a momentary thought that a long bath would be heavenly.

He snorted. Only the sirens who ascended frolicked about in the fountains in Alaxia. He would turn the realm on its head if he splashed beside them.

"Gabriel," Dina stopped just outside his room, sounding breathless. "I need you. Come, quickly."

He sighed. After weeks of slaying demons, he was due a reprieve. "Not today, Dina."

She wrapped pale fingers around his shoulders to face him. "It's urgent."

Something in her words made his chest constrict. She'd been caring for Adalaide while he fought her war. Her only mission of late was to see to her care. If something had happened to Adalaide... But it was what he was waiting for, wasn't it? The thought speared pain through him.

He left the room, following at a clipped pace.

Dina reached the edge of Alaxia and dropped.

He followed, landing on the cobbled street outside Adalaide's home and sucked in a sharp breath as a spasm of pain tore through him, nearly sending him to his knees.

He pushed past Dina, shoving the door open and darted up the stairs to Adalaide's room, falling to her side. She was breathing, the shallow rise and fall of her chest a sign he was not too late, but dark lashes rested heavily against too-pale skin, and he could see no tint of color on her cheeks.

"What happened?"

Dina moved to stand beside him. "She was attacked by six demons at once. She was quite brave, but their poison penetrated her skin. Ultimately, she destroyed them all with her magic, but I fear it was too much. Her physical wounds are healed." She slid back the sheets, revealing two thin scars along Adalaide's abdomen. "But she will not wake."

Gabriel took in her scars. The rise and fall of her stomach. The slow rhythm of her heart and, more disturbing, the faint hum of her soul, clinging to a body that had not determined its fate. His own pain had receded to a dull ache, telling him her soul was intact. But he'd felt nothing until the moment he set foot on the mortal plane.

He hadn't felt it when she was injured. What did it mean? Terror seized him. Had she finally rejected him? Did it break their bond? No. He could feel their connection, weak though it was.

"Leave us." He didn't look up, didn't spare another glance at Dina. He pressed a gentle hand to Adalaide's cool cheek. She didn't move, and her mind was troublingly blank. "Adalaide, don't give up."

Her soul warmed just a fraction, and he knew it was responding to his nearness. He laid both hands on her chest, just over the place where her soul rested and whispered the healing prayer to revive her.

White light glowed under his palms, but she didn't stir. He leaned closer, listening. Her soul hummed a quiet tune. It wasn't singing, not the way it had when they met. It was quietly contemplating what came next.

He whispered the words again, watching as light flared under his palms. Her soul gave a pulse in response. Weak, but it gave him hope. Hope that she would come out of this.

Settling onto the bed beside her, he pressed into her, letting their bodies touch. His flicker of a soul soared at their contact, warming under his skin. He felt her soul do the same.

He slid down on the bed, leaning his head down until it rested against her cheek.

With each movement, each point of contact, her soul warmed, reviving. He draped a hand across her torso and let the gentle rhythm of their souls, syncing with one another, cherish this nearness.

"I never knew I could want to share a part of my being with another. I was certain that the day I met the thief who had stolen it, I would want nothing more than to rip it from them and take back what was mine." He lifted his head, checking to be sure she had not spontaneously awoken to hear his confession.

"I waited thousands of years for the day. I prepared to reunite with my soul in a joyous act and rid myself of the human who sought to take something that did not belong to them.

"These were the dark, insidious thoughts that kept me from the very act. I see it now so clearly.

"The moment I laid eyes on you, I saw the error of my thoughts. I understood why we gave a part of ourselves so you could live. And it's all I want for you.

"I don't want it back. I would give you every last shred of my soul and lay down my eternal life so you could know peace.

"An eternity with me would be torture. A torture I could never want for the only being who has ever truly been worthy of my soul. In my endless darkness, you are the only light.

"Don't go, Light. Find your way back to me."

He closed his eyes, a single tear sliding down his cheek.

Her chest rose steadily, dipping beneath the weight of his arm only to rise again. Her soul pulsed, growing warmer under his touch. It was weighing his confession, considering his words.

Would it choose to be reunited with one who had acted so cruelly? He lifted his head and pressed a kiss to her cheek.

Although her soul was reviving, her body was still.

He rested his head on her shoulder, curling his arm more tightly around her frame and closed his eyes again. Time. She needed time.

And that was something he had in spades.

CHAPTER 22

Gabriel

Days stretched into weeks, and though her soul danced joyfully at each touch, her still form was cool. Dina had come and gone, offering her healing magic; to take his place; prayer. He'd turned them all away.

Adalaide's soul had chosen, but her mind was in a state of limbo.

He'd seen it in mortals before. The soul made its choice to stay or go, but the mind had not, so the body lingered in a form of stasis, waiting for the two to come to terms with one another. In cases where the soul left, the body eventually withered and perished. When the soul chose to stay, but the mind did not, a ghostly echo of their former selves remained.

Helping souls cope with their new state was not something he had much experience with, that was Phanuel's mission.

If her mind chose to leave, but her soul remained, what did it mean for their bond? Would his other half be trapped on the Earthly plane, unable to pass on but unable to bond as well? Would her human body die, leaving her soul behind?

He lay a hand gently on her cheek. At Dina's recommendation, he'd cast a time bubble, allowing her body to remain unravaged by lack of food and water while her mind chose its path forward, but he could only maintain this bubble in time for so long. Its effects would be felt once she woke. *If* she woke.

"Come back to me, Light. The world is dark without you."

Her perfect pink lips were parted, soft breath disturbing the air around her face. As her pale skin flushed under his warm touch, he marveled at how alive she seemed even in this state.

Light brown freckles dotted over the bridge of her nose, and he smiled softly as he noted their symmetry. Lifting his hand from her cheek, he ran a finger lightly over the tiny dots, tracing their shape.

Gabriel gasped, sitting back. The freckles bridging her nose formed the Hyades cluster and splashed over her cheek, Aldebaran sat at the midpoint. He tracked the constellation across her face, swallowing the lump rising in his throat.

Now more than ever, he wished he could wake her, ask her what day she was born, but perhaps the date of her birth was not the lynchpin of the end times. Perhaps it was a girl, marked by the Taurus constellation, sent at the appropriate time, meant to be bonded to the strongest angel yet remaining in Alaxia.

Gabriel stood, moving to the window. Even this small distance sent pain radiating through him. The bond was anxious for them to resolve their connection as if his soul sensed hers desperately in need of him.

He paused, glancing back to her serene form.

Would it be enough to wake her?

The thought of performing the act without her consent made him sick. The fact that he was debating the action left the most vile taste on his tongue. No part of him could reconcile it as an act meant to save her.

It was uncomfortably close to thoughts he had all those years ago of taking back what was stolen from him and discarding the body.

Perhaps a bonding under such circumstances wouldn't take. Perhaps her soul would reject him for even considering such deceit. Humans, after all, had free will. They could choose to reject their bond.

Had she posed it to him directly, he would not have had the option.

Outside her bubble in time, a chill settled on the air, hinting at winter's impending arrival. Soon, the bubble would burst, and one way or the other, time would be up.

A noise at the door had him dissolving from her room to appear in Adalaide's foyer. The noise came again.

Shrugging his shoulders, he draped his wings into an overcoat and slid the door open just enough to peer out.

"Evn'in sir," a man said, dipping his head. His hair was neatly combed, but his shoes were scuffed, and the light odor of metalwork spoke of his profession. Instantly, Gabriel's hackles rose. The man had some nerve calling on an unwed woman at this hour.

"Good evening," he said, raising one brow.

The man swallowed audibly, taking a step back. "I came a call on Miss Graves. Haven't seen her in town o'late, and it's not like the lady. My wife sent me by with a basket. We hope all's well?"

Gabriel's gaze dropped to the proffered basket in the man's hand and the dull band encircling a finger. His anger banked.

"You're too kind. Miss Graves is not receiving visitors presently."

Taking the basket from the man's outstretched hand, he gave a nod and closed the door. He noted with some satisfaction that the man's mouth had dropped open to say more—or perhaps in awe of his grand stature.

In the foyer, he double-checked the wards around the entrance and moved back up the stairs to Adalaide's room, finding her unchanged. He sighed, dropping on the edge of the bed.

Waiting for some change was a torture all its own, but the fear lodged in his chest over what would happen when the bubble burst had his soul pulsing rapidly.

Perhaps he should let it run its course. Wait for the events of her life to play out naturally. If she woke, she would be free to make up her own mind. If she did not, the decision would be made for him. But the pattern dusted over her face was too great a coincidence to ignore.

He longed for Dina's counsel on the matter, but her insistence they bond would only grow exponentially if she believed Adalaide was somehow tied to the sign all beings awaited to usher in the end times.

How could the Naphil lying just beside him, housing half of his soul, be the catalyst that would spark the war at the end of the world as they knew it? He was reading into things. Giving himself excuses to justify his desires.

Another noise at the door drew his focus. The man was relentless. What did he want now?

Gabriel moved to the door once more, flinging it wide.

Eyes in shades of gold narrowed as Sanura hissed and threw up her blood-red nails.

He was frozen in the door, momentarily caught off guard, and it was the moment she needed to dart away. When he'd recovered, he went after her, dissolving into nothing and following her trail.

She was fast, so fast, but he pulled himself along in her wake, letting it lead him back through Cheapside, down the Thames, straight to the estuary and into the North Sea.

He stopped, hovering over the dark body of water as he searched for any sign of her. As it had many times before, her soft blue trail vaporized into mist and was lost to the wind. She must be using the water as her escape route.

When he'd scanned the distance, seeing nothing that gave her away, he turned back, choosing speed, and materialized in Adalaide's room, letting loose a sigh of relief as the pain in his chest receded at her nearness.

Shaking off his disappointment, he crawled onto the bed beside Adalaide in corporeal form and wrapped one arm over her chest. The contact was cathartic, easing some of the tension from his most recent contact with Sanura and further solidifying his resolve.

If a demon had come while he was away or another of Sanura's creatures, they would have slit her throat where she lay, and he would be bereft of his other half until the end times. He'd resolved himself to that fact only weeks ago. Why, then, did the idea spear pain through his chest now?

He rested his cheek against hers, a warm buzz rolling through him. Her soul stretched toward him, begging to be one. Had she been given the choice, she may not have chosen him; after the way he'd behaved, he would have understood if she hadn't. But her soul was of a different mind. It was wholeheartedly committed to the idea.

And why wouldn't it be? It was, after all, his soul. Strange that he hadn't considered it his from the moment they'd met. He closed his eyes, letting his half of their soul stretch tentatively toward hers. The two halves brushed against some invisible barrier—the lack of claiming.

His half smarted at the rebuff, curling back only to reach out once more.

Mine. The single thought reverberated through her mind.

It wasn't soft or tentative. It was loud and commanding. The voice was nothing like Adalaide's. It was their soul speaking through, demanding to be reunited. Every fiber of his being rejoiced, his half pleading for the same.

He pressed his skin against hers more firmly, nestling close, touching in all the ways their souls couldn't.

"Gabriel."

He flew out of bed, landing stiffly beside a bedpost and leaned into it awkwardly. "Dina."

Dina pursed her lips, her gaze traveling to the still form on the bed. "Her condition has not changed."

He nodded, crossing his arms over his chest.

"I have considered our predicament and can think of only one conclusion." He arched a brow, watching as she stalked closer. "You must bond."

Gabriel frowned. He'd been thinking the same, but for her to come pushing her agenda would not be borne.

"Brother," she said, clapping a hand on his shoulder. "She may not wake. If you do not bond with her, she will move on and be lost to you until the end."

"It must be her choice."

"She made it."

Gabriel's chest seized at her words. "What... What do you mean?"

"Before she was attacked, she confirmed she would choose to bond if you would have her." She gave him a look. "I did not tell her the choice isn't ours." She squeezed his arm. "Brother, don't you see? She's already given consent. All that's left is for you to complete the bond."

Gabriel uncrossed his arms, letting them fall to his sides. He glanced sideways, watching Adalaide's chest rise slowly.

"I don't—"

"For heaven's sake, Gabriel. When she wakes, if she hates you, she can reject you in Alaxia." She released his shoulder, moving to sit beside Adalaide.

He turned, watching her place one pale hand against Adalaide's forehead. She slid her hand to his soulmate's neck, feeling her pulse.

"The bubble will burst within the hour. We have no way of knowing what awaits. That she has not woken thus far bodes unwell for you both. Why risk it?"

Gabriel moved to stand behind Dina, watching Adalaide's chest rise and fall slowly. She was unusually still. Humans fidgeted and twitched; they made noises. Everything about her spoke of a body which had given up.

It was a safe assumption she was only still with them because of the time bubble.

Dina squeezed his fingers between hers, pulling him forward.

He came, stopping at the edge of the bed.

"Sit, brother."

He did.

She reached for his other hand and clasped her fingers in his. "Our Father gives us only what we can handle. He presents challenges meant to make us stronger, better versions of ourselves. Only you were strong enough to wait for your perfect match. Only you could survive an eternity alone and still find it in himself to accept that he was worthy when the time was right."

A tear slid down Gabriel's cheek as he took in her open, honest expression and knew she meant it from the bottom of her soul. He nodded, something warming in his chest.

Hope.

CHAPTER 23

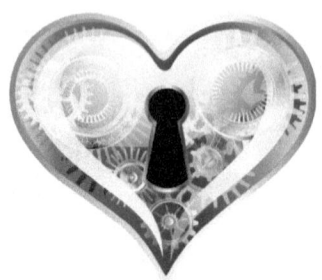

Adalaide

Adalaide blinked, her head aching as though it struggled to contain some new wealth of information. She blinked again, yawning loudly and stretched her arms over her head.

The feel of rough fabric against her skin made her grimace. She had slept in her clothes... again.

She blinked once more, peeling her eyelids open and stared around her familiar room. The walls were a deep green, bisected by dark brown planks, and in each corner was a table with a vase of wildflowers.

The vibrant red of the rose petals was outdone only by its smell, pungent and sweet. Between wild roses were bits of green ivy and yarrow wedged into the vases. Beyond them, out the window, smells of human waste and filth wafted into the room, and on the air, the smell of amusement, anticipation, and contempt also rode in.

The odors were acrid and all at once cloistering. Adalaide jumped from her bed and rebounded off the solid form of a man.

Not a man, an angel. *Her angel.*

Her mind wrapped itself around that thought. He wasn't hers, much as she might have liked to believe it was otherwise.

I am, as you are mine.

The words were a shout in her mind. She pressed her hands to her head, wincing.

"Why are you screaming?" she asked. Her voice was rough and scratchy as though from disuse. She closed her eyes, massaged her temples, and fell back onto her bed. "Please, close the window."

Gabriel turned, dazzlingly white feathers whipping her in the face as he pressed down on the glass, blocking out some of the noxious smell.

He turned back to her, hovering beside the bed. "It will take some getting used to."

"What will?" she asked, rubbing her temple once more.

"Your newly heightened sense."

She looked up, meeting his eyes for the first time. "What do you mean?"

"You have awoken your Nephilim side. Or, rather... that is..."

Gabriel backed away from her bed, putting space between them. She waited for the feeling she normally had when they parted, and it was then she noticed a wholeness within her she'd never felt before. It was as if there had been a space waiting to be occupied, and suddenly it was.

She gasped, rubbing at her breastbone. "What is that?"

Gabriel's face changed, the guarded, wary version of him she was more accustomed to reappearing. "Something has happened."

She waited for him to continue. When he didn't, she prompted, "Go on."

"You were dying."

She raised a brow.

He let out a long sigh, saying, "We have bonded."

Adalaide's breathing hitched for only a moment before her whole face split with a grin.

Gabriel's features softened just a fraction. "You're not angry?"

The apprehension in his tone would have made her laugh if she couldn't hear his unspoken words.

Please don't reject me. Don't leave me.

She lunged forward, letting him catch her, as she wrapped her arms around his neck and squeezed. He held her stiffly as she pressed her nose into his neck and inhaled his mahogany and pine scent. It reminded her of an ancient forest on a rainy day.

A tear ran down her cheek as she pressed herself more firmly into him and felt his feathers tickle her nose.

His arms tightened around her, making her feel safe in a way she couldn't put into words. "I accept you," she breathed; at her words, he squeezed tighter.

Their hearts beat in time with each other, but it wasn't exactly a heartbeat. It was a current of energy running under both of their skins. She could feel it before, but in her new state, the energy between them was alive.

My light in an infinite darkness, he said into her mind.

She pulled back, looking into his eyes. They searched her face, still hesitant, still expecting the worst. She suddenly understood why he'd stayed away. Why he'd tried to put distance between them. He thought himself unworthy. Of her? Or happiness?

"Both," he said aloud this time.

She shook her head, another tear streaking down her face. "How could you think that? You're an angel."

His grip loosened, letting her slide to the floor. He backed up, breaking their connection. "You know nothing of me or my kind. Being a seraph does not make me perfect or good. It means only that I am a soldier in a never-ending war, and you are now shackled to that same fate."

He turned away from her, moving to the window once more. His massive wings hid most of his frame, but the profile of his face was clear as his brows dipped low.

Adalaide padded forward, touching one soft feathered wing, and Gabriel's whole back convulsed in response.

"Don't do that."

His wings curled closer to his back, putting more distance between them.

Adalaide reached forward, trailing a finger down the ridge of his wing, marveling at the softness coating its surface. It was like touching a lamb's ear.

He shuddered. "I said, don't."

Emboldened, she ran her hand over the myriad of sparkling feathers running all the way to the floor. There was an iridescence to them, refracting the air. It was almost as if they glowed. She leaned closer, inspecting the individual feathers that made up each wing.

They were each their own slightly unique color, all in shades of white, and each wing was ever so slightly dusted in silver.

Gabriel spun around, catching her as she nearly collided with his chest.

"I bonded with you to ensure you lived. You are under no obligation to stay or to choose to spend your immortality with me. When you die, you'll be given the choice again. You will have the chance to change your mind."

"Gabriel—"

"You can reject this fate. All humans have free will, and that includes Nephilim."

"Gabriel—"

"You don't have to decide anything now."

"Gabriel, will you listen to me?!"

He closed his mouth, his brows dipping. She may have spoken a bit forcefully, but damn him, he wasn't giving her a chance to speak.

"We don't know each other well, and we come from very different worlds."

He shuffled his feet, his gaze dropping to the floor.

Adalaide pressed a finger under his chin, lifting it to meet his eyes. "I may know nothing of what it means to suffer an immortal existence alone, but I know what it means to suffer a human one. To wake each day and wonder if anyone would miss me if I died.

"I have been utterly and completely alone since the day I lost my parents. I envisioned this as my life until the day you found me. Saved me. Can you imagine? An angel swooping in to rescue me and telling me I'm his soulmate? Me. An unremarkable human with no practical skills." She stifled a laugh, but Gabriel's face remained frozen in that blank mask she hadn't yet learned to decipher.

"What I meant to say was, I want whatever a life with you means. I'm yours."

CHAPTER 24

Gabriel

Gabriel tried to swallow the grin threatening to overtake his face for the third time that day. It had hurt when he left, but it was nothing compared to the agony of resisting the bond. Although the tug in his chest was worse now that his two halves had been reunited, the pain of separating was less.

When she had bared her soul to him, speaking the truths he'd felt for so long, he'd finally understood. She was more than a perfect vessel to house his lost soul. She was the same desolate creature, longing to be made whole. She was his equal in all things.

They had spent the night slipping seamlessly between vocal and mental conversation, and through it all, their unified soul rejoiced.

He had expected it to feel as it had before—when his soul was intact and he'd never known the pain of being torn in two, but it was something new. He never could have fathomed it would feel *better*.

When he left, she'd cried, asking him to stay. It destroyed him. Did his siblings feel this way leaving their other halves? Adalaide understood how important his work was though, not just to her but to all humans. Sanura must be stopped; her creatures ended. Now more than ever, he was invested in the outcome.

He stopped at Uriel's door. "Brother."

Uriel greeted him, grasping both arms. "I hear congratulations are in order."

Gabriel dipped his head. "Thank you. I am here on another matter, though. The reashes in America have reported a surge in nasdaqu-ush. I need all the support I can muster to find their maker and end her once and for all."

"Would that I could, but I am tied up in the war in Syria."

"If I come with you to curb the demon horde in Syria would you follow me to North America to quell the growing nasdaqu-ush population directly after?"

Uriel nodded, wrapping an arm around Gabriel's shoulder. "It's good to have you back, brother."

They left, Gabriel stopping at Dina's door to ask her to look after Adalaide while he was away. She gave her word, voicing her concerns in the same breath.

As Gabriel and Uriel touched down on mortal soil, they were immersed in battle. They fought tirelessly through one week and then the next, healing one another on too many occasions to count. By night, they watched over the humans as the demon populous moved among the soldiers, and both seraphim were helpless to stop them.

Their presence was the only thing keeping the demons from inhabiting and killing by night, and so Gabriel stood vigil beside his brother as thoughts of Adalaide drifted through his mind. He longed to go to her, touch her cheek and hear her laugh, but there was no end to the demons' number, and the battle showed no sign of waning.

It was February or March—he'd lost track of mortal time, and the nights he'd spent waiting for the numbness to wear off could not be counted—when Dina landed beside him.

"She's back."

He sat up, groaning as the latest ache settled uncomfortably, healing too slowly for his liking. "Why are you here if Sanura is there?" he snapped.

"I've managed to drive her off for the night, but you must come. I cannot fight her and her new army alone."

He looked out over the sea of moaning bodies and sighed. The sick and dying were always the ones in greatest need of protection from demons. "You must take my place. Their number is too great."

Dina nodded, and he vanished.

A thrill of nervous tension ran through him. They hadn't seen one other since the night they bonded, and for a human, the time must have seemed long. Perhaps she was angry; perhaps she'd changed her mind. He reached the door and knocked. He wasn't sure why. He could have stepped through her wards and appeared inside, but he was hesitant to overstep their yet undefined relationship.

The door swung open and Adalaide appeared, her cheeks flushed, her eyes sparkling brilliantly.

He swallowed the lump rising in his throat and opened his mouth.

She squealed, tossing the door wide, and threw her arms around him. "You're back!"

He caught her, taking a step into the foyer and squeezing her tightly. For a moment, he held her and inhaled the scent of her very being. Apples and chocolate.

"Welcome home. Would you care for tea? But no, angels don't drink tea. Would you care for..." she stumbled over the words as he released her, and she took a step back.

He grinned stupidly. Was she welcoming him home? They hadn't discussed their living situation and he'd been hesitant to say more on the subject for fear of her reaction, but in this moment, all that consumed him were her thoughts. There were no traces of anger, hurt, regret. She was full to bursting with relief and joy.

Those same feelings warmed in his chest, his soul rejoicing at its other half's nearness. Their two halves met on some invisible plane, wrapping around one another, and he took an involuntary step forward.

Their hands found each other, lacing together. The skin-to-skin contact woke his nerves; they buzzed to life, pulling him closer to her.

Adalaide swayed into him, her small frame pressing into his chest as she lifted up onto her toes and pressed soft pink lips to his.

A riot of emotion burst from her, but her thoughts died, replaced by a single word.

Mine.

He sank into her possessiveness, letting the feeling of their souls melding sweep through him. His whole body radiated with warmth.

He released her hands, wrapping both arms around her and backed her up into a wall, pressing himself firmly against her. His mouth moved on hers, sucking her bottom lip between his teeth and nipping softly.

She gasped into his mouth as her tongue darted out, tasting the blood pooling at the edge of her lip where he'd made a tiny cut. Her eyes narrowed on his momentarily, then they closed, and she repeated the action, biting down on his lip hard enough to draw blood.

Golden liquid dripped into her mouth, mingling with her red blood; he licked it, sucking her swollen lip clean. She moaned into his mouth, and her hands found his neck, yanking him closer.

Arousal swelled between his legs, pressing against her stomach.

He pressed her harder into the wall and released her mouth, pulling back to look at her crimson-stained cheeks and neck. "We should stop."

Her eyes flew open. "No."

"I did not come for this. Sanura is back. We must ward the house before nightfall."

Adalaide's arms loosened from around his neck, and she frowned, a drop of blood welling along the edge of her mouth.

He leaned forward, letting his tongue slide over the seam of her lips where the blood pooled.

Her mouth parted, and she sucked his tongue, letting hers wrap around it. His arousal hardened further, and he groaned, sliding one arm down her back, realizing she wasn't wearing a corset.

Only her thin scraps of fabric and his illusory clothing separated them, and his body was all too aware of that fact. It would be nothing to tear her clothes from her body and press their bare skin together, to let them join in the way their souls had.

She wanted it. The idea of it consumed her thoughts. His were consumed by all the ways she envisioned the two of them.

He groaned again as her kiss became more insistent and her thoughts more explicit. In his long life, he'd never imagined half the things she conjured, some downright dangerous for her fragile mortal body.

He released one arm from her back, finding her hands and pinning them over her head the way she had pictured in her mind, and pulled his lips from hers, leaning down to her neck to plant soft kisses down the tender skin.

He nuzzled her neck, reaching for her hairpin with his teeth and freeing her dark locks. Long curls spilled loose, obscuring his view of creamy skin. He didn't like that. The bond between them urging their skin to be closer didn't like it either.

He released her hands, drawing her hair to the side and pulled her head back roughly, giving him access to her sensitive throat.

Adalaide was panting, her body pressing off the wall to be closer to his. He pushed one hand into the wall, forcing her back, pinning her there just as in one of her several dozen visions. Trailing kisses down her neck, he nudged the white collar of her shirt aside to move south, where the other half of his soul rested contentedly.

When he reached the place where it lay, his soul pulsed in greeting, and he pressed his lips to her breastbone, an overwhelming feeling of rightness overtaking him.

His fingers loosened in her hair, and he pushed off the wall, giving her space.

She leaned into him as he backed up, meeting eyes that were shining. She was... crying?

"What's wrong?"

CHAPTER 25

Adalaide

Adalaide swiped at her cheeks as she moved with him, not wanting their bodies to be parted for even a moment.

"It's nothing."

Gabriel took another step back. "Have I hurt you?" *I'm sorry. So sorry. Didn't mean...*

Fresh tears spilled down her cheeks, and he ran his fingers over them, brushing them aside.

"No. You haven't. I... I didn't want you to be... disappointed."

The confusion written across his face loosened a laugh from her chest.

"It's just that you're... immortal."

When his face hadn't changed, she felt the heat staining her cheeks slide down her neck. Was she going to have to spell it out for him? What was the use of this mind reading if she had to say the embarrassing bits aloud?

"Well, I haven't... lain with a man."

Gabriel's brows rose as his lips parted. The slightest tint of golden blood still stained his bottom lip, and her cheeks flamed. She had done that. She had made him bleed.

He held out a hand. She took it, letting him lead her from the foyer—where they hadn't made it ten steps from the door—to the sitting room and pulled her down beside him on a low-backed sofa.

His wings draped over the top, curling under their feet. "You have nothing to be embarrassed about. Being human is about having human experiences, desires, and thoughts. Never be afraid of what I think of you. To me, you're perfect."

She would have laughed at the absurdity of his words if their truth didn't taste so sweet on her tongue. He meant it with every fiber of his being. Even the strange carnal desires she had that would have made her an outcast in her community hadn't scared him off.

She swallowed, taking in the open expression on his face. "But you're an angel. Isn't it wrong to want to do... those sorts of things... with you?"

Gabriel's mouth did something she'd never seen before. It split into a grin so wide his teeth might have blinded her if they were any whiter. "Do you think angels don't partake in physical pleasure?"

"Sins of the flesh. Isn't that what they call it? Surely, a sin is just that."

"Nonsense made up by humans to keep their women submissive."

Adalaide bit her swollen lip. "But we aren't married."

"We aren't human."

She frowned, mulling that over. What did it mean that she wasn't fully human?"

Gabriel's wings twitched at his back. *It means we don't abide by human laws.*

Adalaide wondered fleetingly if she could simply chuck twenty-three years of human beliefs and begin living as though those rules did not apply. The thought was freeing.

She glanced beyond Gabriel to the bright yellow orb dipping slowly behind his shoulder. It would be night soon, and she had yet to set the wards for the evening.

Hearing her thoughts, he glanced over his shoulder at the setting sun and nodded. When he stood, Adalaide's gaze dropped below his waistband, and she blushed, her eyes darting back up to his smirking face, heat creeping down her neck.

She'd heard his thoughts about their clothes and knew his were only an illusion. Did that mean he was nude? Her gaze dropped again.

Gabriel held out his hand. "Come, Adalaide, let us set the wards for the evening. We can explore the topic more after."

Butterflies swarmed her stomach as she placed her hand in his and felt the warmth in her chest buzz to life at their connection.

Want to feel her pressed against me.

She tried to pull her hands free as his thoughts continued on that path, considering all the things he wanted to do with her, but his grip only tightened as he pulled her into the foyer.

When they reached the entry, he pulled her up beside him. "Let's do it together," he said, lifting their hands to spread an invisible shield of air across the doorframe.

She watched him work and began to do the same, feeling their magic meld together in the same way their souls had. It was beautiful and strong. When they had finished, she collapsed into the chair in her room, sweat trickling down her neck.

Gabriel stopped in the doorway, looking hesitantly around the space. For all his talk of being unlike humans, it amused her that he would choose this moment to pause outside her door.

"Come in," she said.

He stepped through the door, and she sat up in her chair, suddenly too aware of him. The way he turned broad shoulders and even wider wings to move through her narrow door, the way he stood with his back straight, hair atop his head nearly brushing the ceiling, and the stark contrast between his beautiful tanned skin and shimmering silver wings. He stole her breath. He was hers, even if she had done nothing in her short life to deserve him.

Halting in front of her, he held out a hand.

She stretched out her fingers, letting him pull her into his arms. Her breath caught in her throat as he walked her backward to the bed.

The backs of her calves bumped against the frame, and she stopped, looking up into his dark, swirling eyes. The nervous thrum of her heart made her feel hot and cold at the same time, her palms going clammy.

"Tell me you want this," he whispered.

She swallowed. "I want you."

"We don't have to do anything tonight."

She nodded, pulling her hands free from his.

He let her go easily but was close enough she could smell his mahogany and pine scent. His eyes searched her face, and she knew he listened to her thoughts, looking for any sign of hesitation.

How could she explain to him that from the moment she'd laid eyes on him, it was the only thing she wanted? It didn't make sense. It defied logic. When they'd met, something in her—her *soul*—just knew.

She lifted trembling fingers to the buttons on her blouse, undoing them one by one. When she reached her skirts, she pulled the blouse free and finished undoing the buttons. She looked up, biting her lip, and found him watching her.

His eyes trailed her every movement in rapt fascination.

Under his piercing gaze, she felt like a gift he desperately wanted to unwrap. Emboldened, she slid the shirt over her shoulders, letting it fall to the floor.

She reached for the buttons lining the left side of her skirts and began undoing them. The loose skirt slid to the floor, and she stretched her petticoats over one another until she stood in a pile of clothes. Only her undergarments remained.

Gabriel lifted one hand, running soft fingers down her bare arm.

She shivered under his touch but stared boldly, unashamed that she'd foregone her corset again.

He slid her dark curls over a shoulder, revealing her bare breasts.

She bit her lip, watching his gaze travel down the length of her.

His fingers moved lightly over her skin, landing on her cotton bottoms, and he slid them down, exposing her completely.

He moved closer, pressing his warm body to hers. In that same moment, his clothes were gone; skin met skin as he wrapped a hand around her waist and pressed her down onto the bed.

She landed in soft blankets, reveling in their touch against her bare back, but when he came down on top of her, warm skin pressing into hers, she could think of nothing but his touch and every place their bodies met.

It was dark, but the moon cast her room in a silvery glow, making his wings sparkle as they spread around them, cocooning her from the night.

He pressed soft kisses to her neck, trailing them down her body to her thighs. As he slid down, his soft touch tickled her skin, making it come alive with a need she'd never known she possessed.

When his lips moved to the inside of her thighs and began their assent, heat radiated from her core as it pulsed with its own heartbeat. He stopped, looking up from between her thighs, a question in his eyes.

Yes?

He didn't say it, but she heard the question in his mind and nodded, her throat too dry to form a response. Tangling one hand in his hair, she ran her fingers through the silky strands.

His head dipped low, nose running through dark curls as warm breath puffed against the sensitive skin between her thighs.

She tightened her grip on his hair, tugging at it as he pressed his lips softly to the tender area before his tongue darted out and swept along her skin.

She gasped, dropping her head back on the blankets, releasing her hold on his hair, momentarily lost to the sensation of his tongue as it swept up and down, making something coil low in her belly.

Heat burned at the apex of her thighs. She cried out as his tongue moved faster and faster, and then he pressed his mouth to her most sensitive area and sucked.

She wrapped her hands in his hair again, this time scraping against his scalp as her body writhed under his tongue's caress and the tightening in her belly intensified, some foreign precipice dangerously close to tipping.

His mouth lifted, leaving a cold, wet sensation behind, and she moaned for him to keep going.

"Don't stop. Don't ever stop," she begged, but he wasn't listening.

He was climbing up the bed, up her body, pressing his warm length along her thigh as his mouth found hers and claimed her, doing all the same things to her mouth he'd just done between her thighs.

His hard length pressed against her still-wet curls, teasing a new ache in her.

Nothing felt more right than having him inside her this very moment, and she strained against his weight to move her body into a better position underneath him.

He broke their kiss, leaning back. "Has your mother told you anything about the act of lovemaking?"

She shook her head, brushing a dark curl from her face. "No."

His eyebrows drew together. "It will hurt."

She slid her wetness along his warm length, groaning. "I don't care. I need you."

A dimple formed on his cheek as a lopsided grin appeared on his face. "My light is bold. As you should be." *My perfect match.*

She had only a moment to consider his words—he'd called her that before, his *light*, but never aloud—before he was sliding back and something hard pressed against her opening.

He watched her face, moving slowly as he slid inside. There was a pressure, something holding him back, then a sharp pain. He was going deeper, so deep she was sure he would puncture some vital organ if he didn't stop, but the pain was quickly being replaced by a feeling of bliss her mind couldn't form words for, and her soul began to sing with the rightness of their joining.

He pressed a kiss to her lips and she kissed him back, wrapping her arms around his neck, pulling him closer. She slid her tongue between his lips and sucked his top lip into her mouth, tasting him, devouring him, wanting to be in this moment forever.

Then, the hard length of him pulled back slowly, creating glorious friction between her thighs. All her focus zeroed in on that feeling. He was pulling out of her, pulling away, and she opened her mouth to protest, but just as she did, he pushed inside her again, faster this time. Her core pulsed.

He was moving in and out, and her hips were moving with him, acting of their own accord. The pulsing intensified, and her stomach tightened again. His lips found hers once more as he moved inside her at such a delicious pace that every part of her body felt hot and ready to burst.

Something in her chest exploded, and the room lit with a soft blue hue. Her stomach burned, her thighs ached in the best possible way, and the room was a beautiful shade of azure.

"Gabriel," she moaned as he continued to move, making her see stars.

She released his neck and fell back on the bed, gazing at his blue-rimmed wings. "You're on fire," she said dazedly, the aftershocks of an earthquake still rippling through her body.

Gabriel dropped his head into her shoulder, biting her skin gently. It was the tiniest sting, but it sent a new round of pleasure rippling through her.

Adalaide pressed a hand to his cheek.

He looked up, meeting her gaze. Her chest warmed at the pure, contented elation on his face.

"I'm not sure if that's normal," she said, pointing a finger at his flame-rimmed wings.

He glanced over a shoulder and chuckled. The reverberation of his laugh traveled all the way down the length of his still-hard arousal and made her tingle where it vibrated inside her.

"You set me on fire."

"What?"

CHAPTER 26

Adalaide

Gabriel propped himself on his elbows, meeting her stare. "You fed me your fire magic, and as our magic is one, I absorbed it."

Adalaide pressed a hand against his sweat-slicked chest. It was good to know he could sweat, at least. He certainly never seemed dirty or hungry or any of the other human inconveniences she found obnoxious.

Her brow furrowed.

"Witches are the offspring of seraphim. Even though you are of Dina's line, my soul powers your magic. Our magic, like our soul, is one."

"You're saying magic is powered by an angel's soul?"

"More or less."

"And although I have Jophiel's blood in my veins, because we share a soul, it's your magic I wield?"

He leaned in, letting his lips rest on hers. "I knew you were clever," he said against her mouth.

She huffed.

The flames running along his wings winked out, casting the room into darkness. She wriggled under him, feeling him grow harder inside her.

"I imagined it quite differently," she said.

"We have all the time in the world to explore those delicious fantasies of yours." As he said it, he moved, rocking his hips ever so slightly, and her swollen sex warmed in response.

Can we do that again?

His deep chuckling answer sent goosebumps rippling down her arms.

His wings wrapped around them, blocking out the world and its sounds, as their bodies rejoiced in each other's joining, and she cried out his name three more times before they were both finally spent.

Gabriel lifted himself, strong arms pressing into the bed on either side of her. Although they'd lain together long after their lovemaking ceased, the absence of his skin against hers left her feeling cold and melancholy.

He moved silently through the room, and she watched as he turned away from her. Silvery wings, gleaming in the moonlight, hid the full view of his backside.

He returned with a thick navy robe and draped it over her naked body, sitting at the end of her bed.

She sat up, sliding it over her shoulders and scooted off the bed to wrap it around herself.

His pants were back, though his chest was blessedly bare. Her gaze trailed over the expanse of rippling muscles that dipped below his waistline.

"So," she said, "what comes next?"

"Actually..." His pause was long enough that she wasn't sure he'd finish his sentence, but then he said, "I came to tell you I'm headed to America and may be gone a while."

Adalaide swallowed back her first response, which was to call him an arse and throw him out of her house.

His gaze dropped, and she knew he'd heard her thoughts.

"You came here to seduce me before you left?" She'd meant to sound accusing, but it just came out sounding hurt.

"No." He looked up and reached for her.

She moved away, stepping out of his reach. "Why did you come if not for this?"

"I wanted to see you. Before I left."

His wings were vibrating in that way she'd come to realize meant he was upset.

"You got what you wanted. You had better go." She turned away from him.

Strong arms wrapped around her; she couldn't bring herself to pull free. He pressed himself into her back, warmth penetrating the robe and some of her resolve.

"I didn't want this life for you, Light. I tried to fight it. Seraphim are soldiers, constantly called to battle. We have no choice. We must go where we are needed."

Her shoulders softened as she leaned into his touch. Of course he couldn't stay and play house with her. He was an angel. He was fighting for humans. Doing whatever angels did all day. She couldn't be upset with an angel.

He pressed a kiss to the top of her head, tightening his hold on her.

In that moment, she understood those flashes of thoughts he'd had. The war he'd fought with himself. She wished he'd shared them with her rather than keeping them to himself.

Still, she knew she wouldn't have chosen differently, even if she'd known this was how it would be. He would stop in for brief moments in her short life, show her affection, do *that* again, and leave to fight another war to save more souls.

And she would be here. Alone. Just as she'd always been.

Gabriel's arms loosened around her, and he twisted her to face him. "This life is fleeting. When you move on from it, you will be with me in Alaxia forever."

CHAPTER 27

Adalaide

Forever.

It had sounded perfect in the moment, his arms wrapped around hers, their souls singing at the union of their bodies.

Now, she was alone. Alone with her thoughts and her aching heart. This was to be eternity?

In the time she'd known him, they had only spent a handful of days together. And she'd concocted that brilliant plan to convince him to bond with her so she could be tethered forever to an angel.

Why hadn't she asked more questions? Learned more about what eternity with an angel entailed? She knew he was busy, but Jophiel managed to come to see her nearly daily. Jophiel had been with her more days than not.

Why was *she* able to spend her time by her side while Gabriel could not?

When would she see him again? In a week? A month?

It had already been nearly fourteen days. How she'd ever thought that was the pattern he followed was baffling. He came on no schedule, and now that he'd taken what he wanted, she may never see him in this life again.

Jophiel appeared behind her, and she whirled. "You."

Jophiel landed, wiping a hand down her white coat. "Me?"

"What are *you* doing here again? Will Gabriel never come to see me?"

Jophiel's iridescent eyes softened at the edges as she strode forward, clapping Adalaide on the shoulder. "I understand, dear. The life of a bonded Naphil is not easy. But—"

Adalaide tore her arm free from Jophiel's grasp. "But nothing. You can move through space and time to be anywhere in the world you want. He chooses not to see me."

Jophiel opened her mouth to make another excuse for him, but Adalaide cut her off. "Nevermind. You're here to babysit. I've seen or heard nothing from the nasdaqu-ush since our last encounter. Sanura seems to have redirected her attention elsewhere for the time." She waved a hand at the space before her. "Help me set the wards, then you can be on your way."

Jophiel looked as though she may argue, but instead, she dipped her head once before moving up the stairs to begin her work.

Adalaide lifted her arms, preparing the wards downstairs. A faint, cool breeze brushed along the nape of her neck, and she shivered. Something was coming. She doubled her efforts using just a bit of blood magic as added protection, knowing she would need it.

Jophiel appeared behind her, and her brows drew together, forming a vee on her forehead. "Blood magic is not something to be used lightly, Ada."

Adalaide bit her lip. "I find it to be my strongest defense."

The vee in Jophiel's brow deepened. "The cost of using such magic is greater than your mortal life."

Adalaide's gaze drifted to the star etched in blood over her door. "Something vile is en route this night. The wind has spoken of it."

Jophiel moved beside her, staring at the star painted over the door. "Very well. Tonight, we fight, and if you should perish, remember that your death is not the end."

Adalaide swallowed the lump rising in her throat, and the warmth pulsing in her chest gave a tiny spasm. Somewhere, Gabriel knew she was afraid and had sent her a bit of strength.

As if summoned by her thoughts, he appeared in the foyer, dressed in a soldier's uniform, wings draped over his shoulders in the form of a cape. His broad shoulders and face were splattered in green goo, and something dark oozed from a wound at his side.

The wild panic in his eyes banked when he took her in, seeing nothing wrong. "What happened?"

Adalaide slid forward, pulled by some invisible cord, and touched his cheek, wiping a thick smear of mud from it with her sleeve. "You look dreadful."

He barked a laugh, and the tightness in her chest loosened.

You're a sparkling star in the darkest night's sky, Light.

Her cheeks flamed. "I never knew you were a poet."

He grinned, a dimple forming on his cheek, and her heart nearly burst at the sight of it. He wrapped dirt-streaked arms around her, but as they touched, he was transformed into a clean white shirt and breeches, his wings spreading wide in her foyer.

She let his scent envelop her momentarily before pressing him back. "What magic is this?"

Seraph magic. Accessible if you unlock that side of yourself.

She looked up into his dark, swirling eyes. Something flickered over his face, there and gone in an instant. Fear? Yes, she could feel the moment of panic surge through him. He hadn't meant to think those words.

"What do you mean?" she asked aloud.

Jophiel cleared her throat, reminding them she was still in the room.

Gabriel released her, stepped back, and pulled his wings close behind him. "I thought there was danger," he said to Jophiel, stepping forward to clasp arms with her. "I should get back. I'm needed."

Adalaide let out a little grunt. "I've not laid eyes on you in a month, and you've come only to depart?"

Gabriel released Jophiel, looking between the two women. "You're in good hands with Dina."

Adalaide crossed her arms over her chest. "Why can you not stay?"

Jophiel's lips twitched up, but she remained silent.

Adalaide tapped her foot against the carpet, staring him down.

"The humans in America are overrun. Only a handful of my brethren were dispatched to handle the horde amassed there. If I remain with you, things may go very badly for the humans."

"Jophiel can go." *You can stay here with me.* She raised an eyebrow at him, daring him to devise a reason to leave her again.

He gave Jophiel an apologetic look as he wrapped an arm around Adalaide and ushered her from the foyer into her kitchen. She grimaced as she entered the room, averting her eyes from the dark scorch mark staining the floor.

Wrapping his fingers over hers, he squeezed gently. "I am stronger than the rest of them. Where I go, the outcome of a battle is decided. Jophiel doesn't wield my strength in magic or ability."

Adalaide let the warmth in his hands leech into her, giving her strength. "I understand."

"I would be here if I weren't needed so desperately. Even for these moments, countless souls are being lost."

Something sharp pierced Adalaide's chest. She was so selfish, asking him to choose one life over the thousands he was defending.

Hearing her thoughts, his brows lowered. "You're worth ten thousand lives, but—"

"No, I'm not. Go." She cut him off.

His gaze trailed over her face as if to memorize it.

She stared into his dark eyes, seeing infinity in them. "Go," she said again. "We will manage."

He nodded once, bending to press a chaste kiss to her lips. She drank him in, leaning into the kiss and letting her lips part to welcome him. His tongue found her bottom lip, sucking it between his teeth.

The sting, followed by a sharp taste of iron, sent a spasm of heat coursing between her thighs. A dozen thoughts danced through her mind, and she wanted nothing more than to drag him above stairs and have him in all the ways she had imagined.

A cool breeze danced along her neck, ruffling a dark curl. The danger was near; if he stayed much longer, he wouldn't leave at all. She had to let him go. To save the humans who needed his help.

She stuffed those thoughts deep into a dark corner of her mind, hiding them from him.

He released her flesh from between his teeth, sucking her lip clean, then pressed a finger to her cut as warm light glowed softly, the cut knitting itself together. He stepped back, giving them space. The ember in her chest lurched forward, demanding to go with him, but she dug her heels in, letting him go and plastering a serene smile across her face.

His own dark gaze was slightly unfocused, and she caught the lust-filled emotions he was drowning in. A fire ignited in her belly and burned all the way down to her thighs. She pressed her legs together, heat staining her cheeks.

It was easy to block out the fear of what would come later when her own desires were riding her every movement. Perhaps she could take a moment for herself, give in to the feel of him before he was gone again for some indeterminate amount of time.

She lifted up on her toes, pressing her lips against his ear and whispered, "I need to feel you inside me once before you go."

CHAPTER 28

Gabriel

Desire such as Gabriel had never known crashed through him, and he lunged forward, pressing her into the kitchen counter as he closed the distance between them.

Finding the long pin in her hair, he tore it free, letting her hair spill down her back as he slid both hands into her dark curls, tilting her head up to meet his.

He kissed her roughly, devouring her mouth and her yearning and let his illusory shirt fall away as he sucked the very air from her lungs, reveling in every inch of her lithe form pressed between him and the table.

His hips moved, grinding against her layers of skirts, and he wanted nothing more than to tear them from her body and feel their skin unite. A shudder rolled through him as her light fingers slid along the ridge of his wing, his lengthening arousal twitching against her stomach.

Their kiss broke as he bent, tearing buttons from her shirt with his teeth.

Something feral overtook him, and, like a mindless beast, he tore her shirt free and tossed it to the floor, sliding his tongue over the bare skin along her collarbone.

His head dipped further, finding her bare breast—no corset, again—and he sucked the soft pink bud of her nipple, flicking it with his tongue before he bit down, tasting blood.

She moaned, gripping the ridge of his wing.

The feel of her hand wrapped around the sensitive skin made him wild with desire. He released her breast, wholly focused on ripping her skirts free of her body.

He leaned back, finding the waistband and tearing every layer off her body in one fluid motion. He was struck speechless by the perfection of all her ivory skin bared for him—only him. Thin white scars running over her abdomen and under one breast only made her more beautiful.

She was a warrior wrapped in a delicate package.

He grabbed her hips, lifting her onto the counter and growled as she leaned back, spreading her legs wide for him.

The tug of the other half of his soul yanked him forward, and he gave her no warning before he buried himself inside her, letting out one contented sigh before her hips were moving. She slid across the marble counter, muscles spasming around his length, squeezing him tight.

He pressed into the counter, letting her ride him and take her pleasure as he found her hair again, wrapping her curls between his fisted hands and tugging her head to the side, giving him access to the soft skin at her neck.

The bruises he'd made with his mouth before were gone and he wasted no time marking her again.

Her soft, breathy moans turned to ragged panting as she stopped moving, the muscles wrapped around him quivering.

He took up her pace, sliding in and out of her slick wetness and groaned as he felt his own relief nearing.

She dropped her head on his shoulder, digging her teeth into his flesh, and a jolt of fresh desire speared through him, sending his hips rocking forward at a faster pace.

Her nails found his back and dug in, drawing blood.

He tipped his head back, nearly sliding to his knees as release washed through him.

When he had caught his breath, he leaned against the counter, his soul pulsing in answer to her own as their sweat-slicked bodies clung to one another. He opened his eyes and brushed a dark curl from her face.

"Adalaide."

She blinked at him, her bright blue eyes twinkling.

I'm yours for eternity. Please never lose faith in that.

Her soft pink lips turned down. "My angel," she said, touching his cheek. "I will always be yours."

The words chipped away at some long-held fear. In this moment, he believed her. In this moment, he dared to imagine his own happy ending.

CHAPTER 29

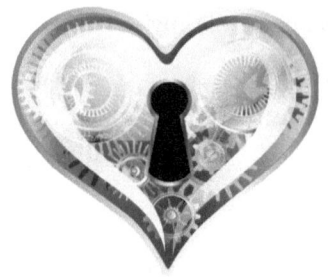

Adalaide

Adalaide buried her dark thoughts in the place only she could see. Gabriel was hers for eternity, as she was his. He'd left his mind open during their lovemaking, and in it, she had seen the truth.

He would have sacrificed everything if she'd asked. He would have traded any mission and the fate of all human souls to stay by her side. She need only say the word. The humans didn't have her promise of eternity. They would die and go to whatever awaited them in the afterlife.

She was guaranteed a future in which her soul would ascend, and she would take her place by his side, her mate. They had forever. She couldn't let him sacrifice the humans for her.

Jophiel rested a hand on her back.

She winced at the still-healing bruise from his sharp teeth. The memory of his bite made her press her legs together. Her cheeks reddened, and she hoped desperately that Jophiel couldn't hear her thoughts as Gabriel could.

"You didn't tell him, but I know you sensed danger."

Adalaide turned, facing the fair-skinned angel. "He was needed elsewhere."

Jophiel nodded. "You are selfless. I'm proud to call you one of my own."

Adalaide frowned. She was anything but selfless. She wanted nothing more than to call him back and keep him with her in her tiny London townhouse, sheltered from the world.

The breeze from before was back, running cold fingers along her neck, and she stiffened. "Someone is nearly here."

Jophiel darted a glance over her shoulder to the door, still marked with Adalaide's blood, and lifted both hands, forming twin balls of flame. They burned in a myriad of colors, looking more like balls of iridescent glass than flame. But when a demon materialized between them, sinking its talons into Jopheils' shoulder, she wasted no time incinerating the creature.

A second demon appeared, and Adalaide cast her own balls of blue flame along her fingertips, tossing fire spears at the insubstantial form before it winked out and reappeared behind her.

She spun, flicking arrows of blue at the creature. An arrow landed directly between the demon's horned brows, vaporizing it.

Adalaide felt pressure on the wards as something sliced a line through one of them. The sound of shattering glass came from the second floor, and she darted up the stairs, casting a ball of flame in one hand and a shield of air in the other.

Jophiel raced after her but stopped halfway up the stairs when the sound of glass breaking in the sitting room drew her attention. She cast an iridescent bubble around her, charging for the sound.

Adalaide had no time to marvel at the creation before two yellow-eyed creatures were on her, teeth snapping for her neck. These were *not* the kind of bites she delighted in. She pressed them back using her air shield and formed a large ball of flame in her left hand.

They gnashed their teeth, caught in a frenzy of bloodlust. She'd been bitten by one of the creatures before and knew they thrived on the blood of humans. Their eyes were glazed as they pressed into her shield, trying to break through.

Quickly, she released the shield, letting them fall into her. She pressed her glowing blue flamed hands into their faces, forcing magic into her palms to melt them where they stood. In moments, they were piles of bones and melted flesh.

She had only a few seconds to catch her breath before something streaked by and a spasm of pain shot through her. She looked down at the bit of splintered wood protruding from her leg and swore. Throwing up another shield, she stumbled back into the wall and forced the shield to spread, encasing her in a bubble of protection.

A blond-haired creature dressed in cobalt robes rebounded off her shield and darted forward, only to bounce off again.

Ignoring the creature, she wrapped blood-slicked fingers around the piece of wood and tugged. White hot pain shot through her and she screamed as her shield of air dissipated into nothing.

The creature charged her again, and she threw up both hands, hissing as the woman's hair erupted in flames, the skin dripping from her face.

Adalaide forced more magic through her fingers, gritting her teeth as the creature slumped to the floor. She slid down with her, sinking against wood-paneled walls and panting, wrapping both hands around the sharp wood protruding from her leg.

Her thigh muscles protested in agony as she bit down hard on her bottom lip and yanked the object free. Fresh blood spurted from the wound, gushing down her leg. She pressed both hands to it, whispering the words to heal herself and whimpered as the soft white light flickered before dying.

"Jophi," she wheezed around the pain.

Jophiel was there, dropping to her knees by her side, cupping her hands over her leg. A soft glowing light burst from between her fingers, and Adalaide sighed as the wound pressed splinters and bits of wood out before sealing closed. Soon, it was no more than a dull ache.

Jophiel glanced at the pile of bodies around her as she stood and held a hand out to Adalaide. "Come. There will be more, I fear."

"What did Gabriel mean by awaken my seraph side?"

"I was not in his head," Jophiel said carefully.

Adalaide recognized the deception for what it was. "Tell me what it means."

Jophiel raised her hands, quickly reinforcing the wards that their first round of intruders had damaged.

Adalaide pressed a hand to her leg and lifted her free hand to assist.

"Save your strength," Jophiel said, glancing back at her.

"Would I be stronger if I woke it?" she tried again.

Jophiel said nothing, silently casting spells.

"Jophi. I may die this night. I'm not ready to die." Her soft words could not hide the quiver in them. "Please, I deserve to know."

Jophiel let her hands fall, turning to give Adalaide an appraising once over. "It does not mean what you think it does. Nephilim are fortunate in that the laws of seraphim do not bind them. They have free will."

"What choices would I lose?"

Jophiel's lips turned down at the corners. "It's more complicated than that. Seraphim may not lie, they may not share the secrets of their kind with others, except with their mate, and most of all, they may not harm a demon unless the demon is inhabiting a human's body or has struck the first blow against a seraph." She beckoned Adalaide forward as she moved from the foyer into the sitting room and motioned for her to sit.

"Seraphim who break these laws are irreparably punished. A lie, even one, results in a permanent marking, labeling them forever as dishonest. To harm a demon who is not inhabiting a human or attacking a seraph results in permanent expulsion from Alaxia and banishment to Primoria. The trip is one way. Seraphim may never leave that place once banished there."

Adalaide tasted the truth in her words and wondered at a life with such severe punishment.

"Would those be the rules I would be beholden to even in... Alaxia?" She sounded out the odd word.

Jophiel's snow-white brows dipped as their eyes met. "These are not my secrets to share. Only your analogous umbra can disclose what immortality means for a soul-bonded mate in Alaxia."

Analogous umbra. She had heard those words before. Another name for soul-mate, Gabriel had said.

"I could protect myself and others if I were stronger."

Jophiel shook her head. "You are Gabriel's. When you leave this plane and ascend, you will be in your rightful place."

Adalaide bristled, heat rising in her veins. "I am no one's. And I wish to be of use now."

"He would never forgive me."

"He would prefer I die?" She wasn't sure why she asked. She'd convinced herself only a few hours before that dying was not that big of a deal, but that was when it was between her life and thousands. Now, when it was only her life or death, she wanted to live. She wanted to fight. "I could be instrumental in stopping Sanura. Do we not want to stop her?"

"More than you know," Jophiel grumbled.

"Brilliant. I can help. Why will you not allow it?"

"If you break our rules, you will be immediately remanded to Primoria. To Hell. What would Gabriel do if you were sent there? He's too strong. If he followed you to Primoria, the balance may tip in *his* favor."

Adalaide's nose wrinkled. "Whose favor?"

"The Fallen."

"You mean Satan," Adalaide whispered.

"Humans have many names for him, but he is our fallen brethren, ruler of Primoria, and the father of demon spawn."

Adalaide grimaced imagining such a fate. "What if I'm already destined for that place? When I die, if I'm not good enough for Alaxia, will I go to Primoria, even as his mate?"

Jophiel gave her a once over as if to say, *What could you have done?*

She swallowed. "I have committed murder."

"You have killed unnatural creatures and demons. Neither of which would stain your soul."

"I killed my parents."

Jophiel paled. "Was it an accident?" she breathed.

"No. Not my father."

Jophiel's luminescent skin dimmed. "Was he trying to kill you?"

"Yes... No. He was distracting me so a demon could do it."

Jophiel closed her eyes. "Ada, this is dire."

Adalaide nodded, biting her lip. "I thought as much."

Jopheil paced the room. "We mustn't tell Gabriel."

Adalaide watched the graceful creature move across the small space, nervous energy thrumming through her. She'd always thought she would go to Hell for her actions, knowing somehow her crimes were too great to be forgiven, but to have it confirmed by an angel made her dizzy.

She wouldn't have forever with Gabriel after all.

"Wait," Jophiel said, pausing mid-stride. "I can make you a reash."

"A what?"

"A reash. It's a second chance only witches are given. When their souls aren't deemed pure enough to pass on to Alaxia, witches, the offspring of seraphim, are given one more chance. They may serve a six-year term in exchange for their souls being wiped clean.

"If they serve faithfully, fight for the cause, and remain pure, they are given back their mortal lives and one more chance to get it right.

"To have this chance, you must be dying, though."

Adalaide bit her lip. "Not a difficult ask, given my circumstances."

Jophiel's mouth pursed. "We've never made a Naphil a reash before. I don't know what it would do to your bond."

Sharp pain spiked through Adalaide. Would she lose the bond? If she was destined to be parted from him upon death, did it matter if there was a chance the bond might be broken when she became a reash?

At the very worst, he would be free of a creature too tainted to be welcome in Alaxia. In the best outcome, she might be forgiven and given a second chance with him.

"I'll do it."

Jophiel nodded slowly, coming to the same conclusion. "It seems to be our best option." She ran a hand across her forehead, pinching the bridge of her nose. "I won't kill you. I can't."

Of course she couldn't. There must be some rule against that.

"There will be more of them this night. When they come, I will ensure I'm injured."

Jophiel's arms fell to her side, and she resumed pacing. "You mustn't actually perish. If you do before I can retrieve your soul, you will not escape your fate."

Adalaide dipped her chin in acknowledgment.

"But if you're not wounded enough, neither can I fetch it from your body."

Adalaide nodded.

"You must be injured in a way in which you will die, but not too quickly."

"I understand," Adalaide bit out.

Jophiel blinked, gazing down at her. "That injury in your leg might have done the trick had we waited a day or two for it to fester."

Adalaide wrinkled her nose. "I'd rather not wait for infection to set in, thank you."

"You're right. A bit of demon poison or a knife to the gut would do nicely."

Adalaide pushed herself off the sofa. "I've had enough talk of my death for the moment. I need tea."

She left the room, not waiting for more instruction from Jophiel on how she might meet her end, and stopped in the kitchen. Her gaze trailed to the dark spot on the floor that marked the place where she'd detonated eight years ago.

She should have had the floors replaced, but some part of her, the part that still sought retribution for her actions, wanted the reminder. She moved to it, standing over the discolored patch in the shape of a starburst pattern.

Her mother's terrified face flashed in her mind. Was she doing the wrong thing? Accepting a second chance when she so clearly didn't deserve one? Try as she might to convince herself she wanted it for Gabriel, the lie sat bitterly on her tongue—a curse. To never be afforded the luxury of half-truths, even for herself. In this, she was like the angels. Perhaps only in this.

She set the kettle to boil and moved along the counter, running her fingers over the smooth surface. The image of her thighs resting atop cool marble flashed into her mind. Her nipples pebbled at the memory of his stinging bites and the way she'd writhed against him, taking pleasure from his body.

It was sinful the way he felt inside her. She bit her lip, flushing as heat rushed between her legs.

The kettle whistled, startling her out of the memory, and she moved quickly down the counter, grabbing a cup, strainer, and the canister of loose tea.

Tendrils of ice danced along the back of her neck. She froze.

The temperature was so cold it could mean only one thing. The red-haired witch was back. Outside this very moment, if her instincts were correct.

She whirled, racing for the front door and slid to a stop beside Jophiel, who was already poised for attack.

"She's outside," Jophiel mouthed.

Adalaide silently lifted both hands. They didn't need to say it. If Sanura was there, this was not the time to be injured. They would need to fight her off if Jophiel hoped to have enough time to retrieve her soul from her body before it expired.

The door rattled as if the witch were testing to see if it was locked. Then a bang sounded, and the door creaked, dangling precariously on its hinges before it tipped backward, crashing to the floor with a resounding thud.

CHAPTER 30

Adalaide

Adalaide shot up in her bed, gasping for breath. She wiped her brow, slick with sweat from another night terror. In this dream, Sanura had come, but this time rather than being chased away by Jopheil's magic and Adalaide's growing power, Sanura had wrapped sharp nails around Adalaide's throat and with her free hand, plunged her fingers through Adalaide's round belly, tearing out her child.

Adalaide had screamed and thrashed but she'd been powerless to stop the vile creature.

Her heart slowed as she sucked in calming breaths, but her throat was raw, either from screaming or retching earlier in the night.

Tossing aside her blankets, she slid two swollen feet onto the floor. Her back ached, but returning to sleep, and more nightmares of the red-haired woman who hunted her, was out of the question.

Groaning, she rested a hand on her round stomach and shuffled down two flights of stairs to her kitchen. Reaching for a glass, she twisted the knob and leaned her full belly against the counter, watching it fill, then lifted the glass to her lips, letting the cool liquid soothe the burn.

"I hope you're comfortable in there my love, for I am quite discontented by your temporary lodgings."

She laughed as the child in her womb gave a small kick.

When she'd learned she was with child, silent terror had stolen through her, but it was quickly replaced with joy at knowing she had made a perfect being with her soulmate. Surely a child born of such love, with one parent of angelic blood and the other a full angel, could be nothing less than perfect.

It also meant she was no longer destined to be alone. She made a silent vow to the child quickening in her womb that she would be a better parent than hers had been. She would be a mother who protected her child even against their father.

Thinking of him sent pain rippling through her and she quickly grasped the emotion, locking it down tightly the way Jophiel had taught her. Where other women prepared for birth in the normal ways—lying in, preparing the home for an infant—she reinforced wards and learned to quiet any emotions that may give her condition away.

It had begun in preparation for her reash transformation, to ensure he did not come and save her before she could transition and have her soul wiped clean. But when one month became three and three became six and the father of the babe whom she'd so adored, never darkened her door, insidious thoughts of her family and her own self-worth crept in.

Now, she cared only about ensuring he did not return simply out of some form of duty or obligation.

Although the pain of his rejection left a deep chasm in her chest, it gave her new resolve. For one fleeting moment, she had dared to hope someone cherished her. And in that moment, she'd given far too much of herself away. When he'd left, taking her innocence and her last shred of hope with him, she'd finally accepted the truth.

In this life, she could rely only on herself, and now, with a child soon to be in her care, she would need to be even stronger.

CHAPTER 31

Gabriel

Gabriel wiped an arm over his brow, resting the tip of his sword in the dirt as he leaned against it. Seraphim didn't need sleep, but they certainly needed rest when they'd been using their gifts for forty-eight hours with no break and the seemingly endless well within them began to suggest there might actually be a bottom.

He looked out across the smoking, burned earth and spied Yomiel wiping a blade against his leg as he sent another demon back to Primoria. Days had jumbled together, and only the memory of Adalaide's soft skin, flush with his and his name spilling from her lips, kept him sane.

Around him, men carried makeshift stretchers as they sifted through the dead for the ones who clung to life.

Now—in the moments when only moans of the sick and dying permeated the air—was when demons mounted their attack. They dived on the injured, sucking their misery from them, pressing into their bodies only to bask in those final precious moments

Between a mass of bodies crumpled over one another, he spied a dark form slipping in and out of their gaping mouths: a wraith drawing energy from their

136

last breaths. They could always be found around a battlefield or a hospital. They hastened men's demise, stealing their final moments.

He pressed into his sword, stepping over prone forms, some with torn limbs, others with dark stains across their chests or heads, stopping in front of a pile of lifeless bodies. He lifted his sword, waiting for the moment when the wraith would materialize once more.

A dark substance dripped from a man's nose, pooling just in front of Gabriel. He waited for it to be material enough to vanquish; as it solidified, a dark gleam settled in its red eyes.

"Astaroth," he seethed, swiping at the demon.

"Ssseraphim," Astaroth hissed, dodging the blow.

"What are you doing here?" Gabriel demanded. "Don't you have more important tasks to attend to? Surely your king does not find human battles worthy of his general's time."

Astaroth's red eyes narrowed. "I am here to give you a messsage."

Gabriel straightened. "What is it?"

"My king sssays you have found your mate at long lassst."

Gabriel lifted his sword, prepared to strike.

Astaroth brought up smokey, insubstantial arms. "He wissshesss to make a deal."

"What deal."

"Hisss mate for yoursss."

Gabriel's chest seized. He couldn't have her. Gabriel would have known. He would have felt it. As if in answer, the warmth inside him pulsed. She was alive, still on the mortal plane.

"He is in no position to make such a bargain."

"Hisss mate wishesss her dead. When Sssanura wants sssomething. Ssshe getsss it."

It was true. Gabriel had never been able to stop her. In three thousand years, she had always managed to elude him.

"What does he want from me?"

"There isss an amulet. Give it to her, and your mate goesss free."

"I don't have any amulet."

"But your mate doesss."

"What does she want with it?"

Astaroth shrugged, his wispy dark shoulders going solid for a moment. Gabriel swung his sword, but Astaroth turned to smoke, and the sword sailed through air.

Astaroth gave him a dark glare, his red eyes narrowing. "Ssshe hasssn't much time. Do you agree to hisss bargain?"

Gabriel sheathed his sword, saying nothing as he vanished.

He landed outside Adalaide's home and materialized inside her foyer. It was dark and unnaturally still. He checked her wards, ensuring they were whole.

"Adalaide," he called in the dark silence.

Light flared to life above, and he rushed up, taking the stairs two at a time.

She came to the edge of the stairs as he reached the top and folded her arms over her chest, her mouth set in a grim line.

"What are you doing here?" she whispered.

"I came to see you." *What do you mean?*

He searched her thoughts, but they were silent. Blocked or hidden.

"Adalaide." He held out a hand.

She dropped her gaze to his outstretched fingers, then trailed it back up to his face. "You have been gone a long time."

He fumbled for the right words. It had been a few months. He'd been busy. There was a time when he'd needed two siblings to heal him, and he'd had to go to Alaxia to recover. He should have come; he knew he should, but it hadn't been that long. Had it?

Twelve months.

He stepped back, the words nearly shouted at him. "No. It was... two, maybe three."

"It's been twelve months. It may not seem like much to you, but... for a human, it is a long time." There was pain in her eyes.

Light. My light. He dropped his hand, feeling foolish for leaving it outstretched so long. "I'm sorry."

The pain in her eyes sharpened into anger, and she let another thought slip through.

Too late for that.

She turned away from him, but he caught her arm. She spun back, pure outrage painted across her face. "Remove your hand from me, sir." The venom in her words stung.

He released her, taking another step back.

A sharp wail pierced the air.

He darted a glance toward the sound, then dropped his gaze to her midsection. Their eyes met, and hers were round. He bolted past her, straight for the sound.

"Gabriel, wait."

He stopped at the edge of the door. The sound came again from a bassinet at the center of the room. His feet moved, bringing him closer. Every nerve was alive as he approached. He peered down, unable to move or speak. In a small pine crib, nestled between crisp white linens, were not one, but two miniature humans.

One, the one who had given them away, opened his mouth and let out another startlingly loud scream. Warmth spread through Gabriel, thawing his limbs. He leaned down and picked up the tiny creature. The baby squirmed in his arms, making pitiful sounds.

He felt her as she moved beside him, gazing at the beings they had made. As if sensing his brother was gone, the other began to sniffle.

Adalaide leaned down, picked him up, and cradled the perfect cherub in her arms.

"Why didn't you tell me?" he whispered.

She scoffed, twisting away from him and marching across the hall to her room. She laid the baby down gently and slid onto the bed beside him, wrapping her arms around him as she yawned.

Gabriel stopped in the doorway, his gaze moving between his other half, stretched out on the bed, and the tiny form in her arms.

She closed her eyes, humming softly to the infant until his plump lips parted and small noises drifted from him.

The baby in his arms had quieted, but he wasn't sure what to do with him. Should he take him back to his crib or bring him in? Back. Back seemed like the best option.

"Don't. He'll only scream for his brother. Bring him to me."

Gabriel hesitated in the hall, frozen with indecision.

"Bring him before he wakes."

Her sharp tone cracked like a whip, and he jolted forward, moving into the room. He settled the child into the blankets beside his twin and studied them both.

"They're perfect," she agreed, hearing his thoughts.

He looked up, taking in her bright eyes and the dark circles now rimming them. "Adalaide. I didn't realize..."

She stared at him for one long moment, weighing something before she let out a breath and her head fell back on the pillow, as she closed her eyes once more. "Stay or go. I'm quite tired and will need to be up in a few hours to feed them."

"I must speak with you. It's important."

She laughed mirthlessly. "I have no doubt if it brought you to my door."

"Adalaide, I'm sorry. Truly. You don't know what it's like for seraphim. I would have come had I known."

Her eyelids never cracked as she said, "Tell me your important news so we may both return to our lives."

He hadn't thought he'd long for the anger or the bite, but the complete lack of emotion was worse. He moved around the bed, sitting beside her and rested a hand atop hers. Warmth bloomed in his chest, his soul rejoicing at their reunion.

He knew she felt it too, but she gave no outward sign of it. In fact, her breathing had deepened. He leaned closer, inspecting the slow rise and fall of her chest. She was asleep.

Huffing a soft laugh, he slid down beside her, letting his wings drape over the edge of the bed, pressing his body against hers. A deep aching hollowness he hadn't let himself acknowledge slowly began to recede as their one soul reached out, merging, welcoming him home.

CHAPTER 32

Gabriel

He hadn't slept. Seraphim didn't sleep, but he'd settled into a quiet, contented calm, giving himself time to recharge and his soul time to recover from their separation.

Alone with his thoughts, listening to the steady breathing of not one but three other people, he'd given himself time to truly examine his actions. He hadn't known how long he'd stayed away, but he knew it was a conscious decision, at least on some level, and he wasn't sure if she would forgive him for it.

Soft snorting sounds were beginning as the blankets were ruffled around. Gabriel sat up, smirking at the miniature human wrestling to be free of the blankets he had wrapped his arm in. He lifted the blanket, freeing the babe just as the other infant punched him in the arm.

"Hey," he said, giving him a playful punch back.

An ear-splitting wail erupted from the small being and he winced, lifting his hands in a placating gesture. "Sorry, sorry. Shh. shhhhh. Don't wake your mother."

"Too late," she groaned. The words—a repeat of the night before—sent a spear of pain through his chest.

"I'm not awake enough for your feelings this morning. Please make tea."

Gabriel stood, slinking from the room and the two bawling infants. He ducked through the doorway and into the hall, sighing as he put space between himself and their deafening shrieks.

In the kitchen, he pulled open drawers and cabinets, searching for the items needed to make tea, and he frowned. Thinking back to the last time they'd been in the kitchen brought images of her naked body sitting atop the very countertop he rested his hand against and the feel of her as she moved, her warmth wrapped around him.

Don't even think about it.

Her thoughts made him wince. *I can't seem to find the tea.*

In the canister labeled "tea".

He scanned the counter and shook his head reaching for it. He found the teapot and the strainer after a bit more searching and no other help from her.

Going slowly up the stairs, he balanced a cup of tea, sugar, wafers, and fruit on a tray. He stepped through the door and stopped.

Adalaide looked up, giving him a tentative smile. Cradled in her arms, tiny mouth latched to her bare breast, his child drew strength and energy from his soul's other half.

In that moment, something inside him changed. He could understand why humans sometimes gave up everything for their offspring, laying down their lives or making bargains in exchange for the small helpless creatures they'd made.

He moved into the room, bringing the tray to her bedside table and setting it down.

"Thank you," she said, looking up at him.

He sat at the edge of the bed, transfixed.

Her cheeks were flushed with color, and he didn't know if it was from her nudity or something else. He couldn't tell what she was feeling either.

"How are you blocking me?"

Her cheeks flushed a deeper pink.

"Jophi has been teaching me."

"She has no right to interfere in our business," he grumbled.

The soft smile working its way across Adalaide's face vanished. "She was helping me. I cannot say the same of you."

He slid closer to her on the bed, letting their thighs touch. The warmth bleeding through the blankets made his soul sing. He had truly been gone too long. "How is blocking me from your life helping?"

Adalaide let the babe in her arms—asleep again—slide back into the blankets beside his brother. She pulled up a bit of fabric over her shoulder, covering herself and scooted back on the bed, moving away from him.

"You left me alone. Do you have any notion of what it's like to fight demons and night-creatures when you're round with not one child, but two? Sanura and her creatures came for me on too many occasions to count."

The pain lacing her voice was a spear through his chest. He lifted a hand to touch her cheek, but she turned her face, swiping at a single tear.

"On the nights when I wasn't heaving up my guts from the nausea of pregnancy, I was fighting for the lives of myself and our unborn children. On the rare night when neither was tormenting me, the ache in my chest at your distance or whatever pain you were enduring..." At this, she choked on a sob.

Gabriel inched along the bed, moving closer to her once more, and wrapped a tentative arm around her. He thought she might pull away, but this time, she didn't, letting him wrap her in his embrace.

Her choked cry became a soft whimper as she leaned against his shoulder. Wet tears soaked into his arm as she cried softly, and he held her.

He pressed his cheek to her soft curls and squeezed her tightly to him. "I was afraid. It's no excuse. I know."

"Afraid of what?" Her reply was muffled by his arm.

How could he put into words his fears? He couldn't, he realized, so he showed her instead, letting all the things he'd held back when they were together dance across his mind. Millennia alone, watching all his siblings find their analogous umbras and connect or, in rare cases, not.

Thousands of years of hope, not for someone to share it with, but to be reunited with the part of him that had been stolen. His plan to take it back, to rip his soul from the woman who would be gifted a part of him.

She said nothing, listening to all his chaotic, jumbled thoughts as he let them spill into her mind.

He moved forward to the moment they had met, the guilt and pain over all those centuries of plotting. The fear that he wasn't worthy of a creature as perfect as her. The way the darkness had begun to consume him until her light had erased it.

He shared the memory of the day he'd almost taken the elixir that would relieve him of all those feelings.

Her tears dried, and slowly, the wall in her mind crumbled. Emotions peeked through. Terror, fear, sadness. Not because she was stuck with such a selfish, unfeeling being, but for all he'd suffered and at the thought of losing him to his darkness. His chest warmed.

"I didn't deserve you. Didn't know how to be what you needed. Didn't feel worthy of the joy you brought me." His arms loosened as she tipped her head up to look into his eyes. Her piercing blue gaze searched his face. He swallowed and went on. "I never thought of what it did to you to be parted." *Selfish*, he thought, but didn't say.

Adalaide wriggled out of his embrace and lifted her arms, wrapping them around his neck. *You needed this hug more than I did*, she said into his mind, squeezing.

Reveling in her touch and her unspoken forgiveness, he vowed to them both he wouldn't leave her to face life or her afterlife alone again.

CHAPTER 33

Adalaide

Jophiel appeared just before dark and dropped to the floor in the least graceful manner Adalaide had ever seen the angel comport herself. She smothered a giggle.

"Brother," Jophiel said, crossing the room to clasp his arm when she had recovered from her momentary shock. He maneuvered Henry into his left arm and wrapped his fingers around her forearm in greeting. "It's good to see you here," she said, darting glances between Gabriel and Adalaide.

Adalaide nodded in confirmation of the silent question on her face.

"I am here to watch over them now, sister. You may resume your place in America."

A wide grin broke over Jophiel's face. "That's excellent news."

She gave Adalaide another look as if to confirm one last time before she dipped her head and vanished.

Adalaide hadn't known what to expect when Gabriel stayed through the morning and the rest of the day. She hadn't expected such a doting father. The boys hardly cracked one tiny lid before he was there, picking them up, cooing over them, or rocking them in his arms.

If she hadn't already forgiven him after seeing his thoughts, she would have done so the first time he picked up a babe and held him close. Who knew an angel could be such a loving parent? His attention had mercifully granted her reprieve from tending to two infants, and she had slept half the day.

Now, she felt restored in a way she could only remember feeling in blurry, distant memories.

She moved John from her left arm to her right and went to the lounge in the back of her home to sit. They'd erected the evening wards early, and now they were left with nothing to do but wait.

Gabriel came into the room carrying Henry and sat across from her. "I need to speak with you. I had put it out of my mind with everything," he glanced down at the baby cradled in his arms, "but…"

She pulled her thoughts from the buzzing warmth in her chest as she watched him holding their son. "Yes, your news. What is it?"

"Do you have an amulet of some kind? A family heirloom?"

She swallowed as all warmth in her evaporated. As if it had heard, the object pulsed against her breast. "Yes."

"May I see it?"

She cleared her throat, shifting John to her right arm, and lifted trembling fingers to her neck. She hadn't thought to remove it before, but there must be some punishment for having a dark object such as this. She should have removed it, burned it, but it had been the only thing she had left of her parents, and it was the one thing they had both agreed on. The amulet was to be protected at all costs. If it ever fell into the wrong hands, it could have dire consequences.

She slid the amulet out from under her clothing. The place where it had touched her skin felt empty and cold.

Something in Gabriel's eyes flashed. "The Amulet of Endor," he said, sucking in a breath.

"What?" She ran a finger over the chain absently; it warmed under her touch.

"Adalaide, that necklace is dangerous. Why do you have it?"

There was no judgment or reproach in his voice, only genuine concern. The tension in her shoulders eased a fraction. Perhaps this wasn't about judgment for her actions after all.

"My family has been charged with guarding it. I am the last."

"Do you know what that thing houses?"

No, but I know it is evil, she said into his mind.

Why did you keep it?" Again, no judgment.

"No one could keep it as safe as I could."

Gabriel's brows dipped as his voice turned sharp. "Does the necromancer know you have it?"

"Yes."

He shot to his feet, rocking Henry as he moved for the door. "We'll need to reinforce the wards to ensure she doesn't get it. If she gets her hands on that amulet, she will resurrect herself permanently."

A tremor racked Adalaide's fingers. What would it mean for her boys, for the world, if Sanura was no longer trapped in a body which could only terrorize them at night? Suddenly, she understood why it had been so important that her family protect it.

"It would be worse than you can imagine," Gabriel said, hearing her thoughts. "She only possesses a fraction of her power now. With her Nephilim form restored, she would be virtually unstoppable."

Adalaide's gaze fell on the sleeping child in her arms. "It's no longer just me she is after. She wants to end my line. Our boys are in danger."

Genuine fear shone in Gabriel's dark, swirling eyes as he looked between the two babies and back to her.

"I must end her. It's the only way to keep you safe."

He crossed the room, settling Henry into the bassinet she'd set up downstairs for the nights when she was too exhausted to carry the boys above stairs before turning back to her, his lips parting.

"You promised," she whispered.

"It is the only way to keep my promise," he said. The words were laced with such conviction she knew nothing she said would change his mind. He nodded, seeming to take her defeat as acceptance and disappeared just as Henry began to wail.

CHAPTER 34

Gabriel

Gabriel appeared beside Dina on the battlefield and unsheathed her sword. "You'll need this," he said, handing it to her.

"Why are you here? Who is protecting Ada and the boys?"

"I can protect them best by ridding the world of Sanura once and for all."

Dina's iridescent eyes narrowed. "You left her once, and she forgave you. If you leave her again, she may not have you back."

"I'm not leaving her, sister. I'm keeping her safe." He rubbed absently at the ache in his chest. Every time he left, even when it was for a cause such as this, the pain was immediate and consuming. He'd learned to push through it and that it lessened with great distance and time, but it was a dagger to his soul every time they parted.

"And what if Sanura finds her first? What if she kills your soulmate and offspring while you rush off to play hero?"

He shook his head, and the unsettling picture she painted departed his mind. "It won't come to that. I will find and end her."

Dina gave him a sorrowful look. "Your sons are not Nephilim. They have no seraphim to bond to. When they die, their souls will ascend to the human fields to await the end times. Will Adalaide forgive you for parting her soul from theirs so young?"

"It won't come to that. I'll protect them, and they will have long human lives. All of them. When it's time for her to pass on from this world to Alaxia, she will be at peace."

He didn't wait to hear more. Dina didn't understand. How could she? Her only child had lived a long human life and now resided in Alaxia with her mate. Dina could visit her any time she liked. She didn't understand how it would torment Gabriel to lose his sons to the field of human souls after meeting them only once.

He would do whatever it took to ensure that didn't happen, even if it meant risking Adalaide's wrath. She would understand. Eventually.

He landed in Alaxia and strode quickly for Raphael's room. Stopping in the arched doors, he cleared his throat as Raphel hummed along to his mate's soft strumming of her harp.

"Raphael, Mary." He said by way of greeting.

They looked up, matching smiles on their faces and said in unison, "Gabriel."

Gabriel slid his tongue along one sharp tooth to calm his nerves before saying: "I come seeking assistance."

Raphael threw his leg over the bench and marched toward him, clapping a hand on his shoulder. "I am yours. Name thy request."

"I'm searching for Sanura."

Over Raphael's shoulder, Mary made a shrill sound of protest. She came to stand beside her mate and wrapped her arm around his waist. "She's dangerous, Gabriel. Think you not it best to seek Michael or Chamuel's aid?"

He ignored her, saying to Raphael, "She threatens my mate's life."

Raphael gave Mary a sheepish grin, shrugging his shoulders as some silent conversation played between them. She released his waist, crossing her arms over her chest. He leaned down, kissing her forehead as she glared up at him.

He searched her face for a moment before turning and ushering Gabriel out the door.

Gabriel spared one backward glance for a glowering Mary before he followed Raphael, who was moving quickly.

"It feels an age since we've adventured together, brother!" Raphael said excitedly.

Gabriel refrained from commenting on Mary's mood, understanding somewhat better now what might await Raphael when he returned.

When they reached the holy armory, Raphael slid a massive sword from the wall and strapped it to his illusory scabbard. Next, he grabbed twin maces, holding one in each hand. "Ready," he announced.

Gabriel moved along the wall, selecting a row of daggers that he slid under his own illusory band around his waist, and reached for the spear he'd used for more than nine centuries before taking Dina's flaming sword on his quest to end the nasdaqu-ush.

It felt good in his hands, like an old friend. Though her sword's ability to absorb flame had made it useful, the spear worked beautifully with his air magic, allowing him to send it great distances through his enemies' corporeal forms.

"Let's go," he said, leaving the room and Alaxia in search of Sanura.

CHAPTER 35

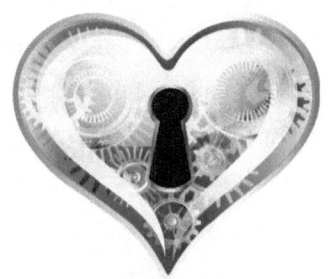

Adalaide

"I said I was certain," Adalaide gritted through clenched teeth.

Jophiel gave her another look of apprehension, staring down at the bloody wound in Adalaide's middle.

"We agreed to wait until the babies were born, but every day I put it off is a day closer to Primoria." She gasped on the words, sucking in pain-filled breaths.

She was focusing all her energy on blocking any emotions from Gabriel. If he came before they had a chance to do it, he would heal her, and their chance would be lost. It had taken all her focus to block those thoughts from him when he came. She wasn't ready to let him know the truth. That if she died, she would not end up in Alaxia.

Her strength waned, and she pushed all her energy into blocking him as her heart slowed. "Do it. Before he senses my distress or pain."

Jophiel nodded and disappeared.

Adalaide pressed both hands to the stabbing pain in her chest. Dark blood slid between her fingers as they loosened and her strength depleted. *Hurry,* she thought as she slipped from consciousness.

Adalaide blinked. It was dark, and something ached in her chest, but when she pressed a hand to the place where the demon had stabbed her, it was solid and whole. No scar tissue marred the surface of her smooth skin. It was as if they had taken her out of her battered, dying body and placed her in a new one.

She got to her feet, marveling at the lightness in her step. She felt restored. As if years had been taken off her life.

Then, a brilliant white light, blinding in its intensity, swallowed the room, and an ethereal voice spoke. "You have chosen well, Adalaide Graves, and for this, we shall bless you."

She squinted, holding up a hand to shield her vision.

"Your sacrifice will mean a great deal to the humans."

Was it God? Had he come to wipe away her sins? She bowed her head as a flaming sword dropped to her side.

The glow in the room diminished, the sword's flame winking out. She reached for the handle, feeling its weight in her palm. Looking up, she glanced around the darkened room, giving her eyes time to adjust. She was surprised to find they did not need it. She could see perfectly in the dark.

The sword hummed, and it was her only warning before an inky black substance detached itself from the corner, red eyes blinking open as it dived. She swung without thinking, slicing through its middle. A thick spray of green coated her before the creature misted out of existence.

She spun in a circle as someone else landed behind her.

"I apologize for the theatrics," Jophiel said, running a hand down her pristine white overcoat. "Zadkiel can be a bit dramatic about the whole thing."

Adalaide peered beyond Jophi but saw no one.

"He has gone. He has little interest in spending time among mortals."

Adalaide nodded, wiping the green goo coating the sword on her skirts and lifting a hand to her cheek. "It burns."

"Come, we must wash it off before it takes off your skin," Jophiel said, ushering her toward the kitchen.

Adalaide went, setting the sword down on the marble counter as she undid the buttons on the sleeves of her blouse and rolled them up. She reached for her bar of soap and twisted the faucet.

"Stop!" Jophiel extracted the bar of soap from her hand and scanned the counter. "Do you have salt?

Adalaide frowned but pointed to a canister labeled "salt" beside the others.

"Right," Jophiel said, unscrewing the lid and scooping out a handful of the grainy substance. She lifted it to Adalaide's cheek and rubbed rough granules over stinging skin. When she finished, she pointed to the running water. "Now, you may rinse."

Adalaide obeyed, letting the cool water run over her skin.

Jophiel twisted the faucet and handed her a towel.

She patted her cheek, eying the angel as she busied herself cleaning up the mess. "What do we do now?" she asked.

Jophiel's wings twitched, giving off a bit of an iridescent glow Adalaide hadn't noticed before. As she gazed at the long white feathers laying layer upon layer, over one another, on the angel's back, she noticed for the first time that there was a faint glow edging them.

It trailed up the ridge of them and ran upward, forming a delicate circle around her head.

"Is that a halo?" she asked incredulously.

Jopheil touched a hand to her head. "It's the sign of my completed bond."

On instinct, Adalaide touched the top of her own head.

Jophiel smiled. "Only full seraphim receive them. And only after the bond has been completed in Alaxia."

The words struck a memory in Adalaide—something Gabriel had said or thought once about her having another chance to change her mind later.

"I'm not truly bonded to him then?"

"No."

Her shoulders sank. "Oh."

"You must accept him again after your final death."

She'd been afraid of death before, nervous about the afterlife and what it would mean, but with two small infants dozing above stairs who were reliant upon her for survival and a witch after them, she couldn't imagine giving up her life now and leaving them unprotected.

Gabriel hadn't returned. She doubted he'd realized it had been another month; he had no concept of human time. It soothed some of the pain she felt at his long absence, but she couldn't hope he'd do better at caring for their children if something happened to her.

"Gabriel told me it's the amulet she's after. What if I got rid of it? Or," she swallowed, "gave it to her?"

Something in Jophiel's eyes flashed. "You must never return the amulet to her. She would kill you the instant she had it to ensure no one could ever trap her again."

"I don't understand. What have I to do with it?"

Jophiel gave her an appraising stare. Indecision warred on her face before she said, "Come, let me tell you the story of your ancestors."

They moved to the sitting room, each taking seats on opposite chairs when Jophiel began.

"Three thousand years ago, there were many Nephilim. One family, the one descended from my line, was more numerous than most. My mate's family name was Gavras. As I had Mary, she, too, had children who were born Nephilim, and so the line continued, and nearly all the children of my line were Nephilim for two centuries.

"Sanura came into her power at the same time my great-granddaughter Helena did.

"But where Helena used her gifts for good, protecting the people of her city, Sanura used her dark gifts to wage war in the name of her analogous umbra.

"When it was discovered who her mate was, I, along with Raphael and several others, entreated with our Nephilim offspring to put an end to her.

"Several members of my line drew on their gifts to end her and send her to Primoria, where she should have remained for eternity with her soulmate, but she was not content to remain below. She wanted revenge.

"Using her gift of necromancy and the Fallen's own gift to create a reash, she was restored to her human form. Her sole mission was to exact revenge on those who had slain her.

"Over countless decades, they fought, but each time she was killed, she resurrected once more.

"The Gavras family devised a new plan. She was captured, her finger severed, and the amulet was created. With the bone of her finger encased in a mixture of gold and the blood of my line, the Gavras family placed a spell upon the amulet that would prohibit her from resurrecting when they ended her one final time.

"Sensing her imminent end, she escaped them and built an army of nasdaqu-ush, more determined than ever to end the only line who could use the amulet to ensure she was killed once and for all.

"Though they have dwindled in number over the centuries, my line has made keeping the amulet safe their one mission until such time as we can finally end her."

Adalaide considered her words, tasting their truth. Something rancid followed as an aftertaste.

"What have you left out?"

Jophiel laced her fingers in her lap, looking down. "I cannot tell you all of it."

"Why?"

"Gabriel wouldn't want me to."

Adalaide scoffed. "Gabriel isn't here. He rarely is. What has he to do with it?"

Jophiel's hands tightened in her lap. "I shouldn't say."

Adalaide blew out a breath. "Jophi, he may return in another year. I could be dead by then, and who would look after my children? Tell me what you're keeping from me that I might keep them safe."

Jophiel's wings gave a little twitch, and she sucked in a deep breath. "To end her and ensure she remains dead requires a sacrifice from the blood of my line."

CHAPTER 36

Gabiel

Gabriel landed in Alaxia and stalked down the long, gilded hall of chambers. He reached her room, not bothering to stop in the doorway. Marching to her silhouette framed in the window, he grabbed her shoulder, spinning her around.

"What have you done?"

Dina turned, eyes glistening. "I had to."

"What. Did. You. Do?" He bit out each word even as he longed to take his spear and run it through something, anything.

"It will ensure she can never harm them," she pleaded with him. "Your sons will be safe. The rest of the humans will be safe."

"You had no right!"

"She will be here with you. You were set on that fate. What has changed, brother?"

Gabriel released her shoulder, letting his hands fall to his side as he clenched his fists hard enough that gold slid between his fingers and dripped to the floor.

He had never dreamed of inflicting pain on one of his own, but in this moment, he could think of nothing that would bring him greater satisfaction than to watch the light drain from his sister's eyes.

"First, you made her a reash without telling me; now you have bound her to another of your ridiculous spells. This will be undone. You will undo it."

Dina stepped back, her wings hitting the wall. "I... can't. The magic accepted her sacrifice."

He roared his fury. "You made a deal with the devil!"

"I didn't."

"You may as well have. He is the only one who can release her from this fool's bargain you made."

"She wanted this. She gave it willingly."

"At your behest."

"Gabriel, I'm—"

"Save your apologies. I will make this right." He turned on his heel, storming from the room.

He landed hard beside the makeshift tents filled with the dead and dying.

Scanning the shapes moving through the dark, he spied the one he had come to find and landed beside the cot of a dying man just as Astaroth materialized outside his body.

"I wish to speak with the Fallen."

Astaroth eyed him like a cat, slanting red eyes in his direction before his smokey lips twisted into a dark grin. "Change your mind, angel?"

"It's my business. Will he entreat?"

Astaroth's horned brow rose a fraction. "Doesss it pertain to the amulet?"

"He will want to hear what I have to offer."

Astaroth bobbed his head once and disappeared. In moments, he returned. "He will meet. One week from tonight in the old temple to Zeusss."

Gabriel nodded and dematerialized, solidifying outside Adalaide's townhouse. He pushed through the wards, opened the door, and stepped inside.

"I won't bother asking where you've been or how long you'll stay," a voice said in the dark.

He opened his mouth, but she continued speaking.

"Jophiel told me you're upset with my plan. If you've come to change my mind, please save your breath. I have made my decision."

He moved in the dark through the foyer and into the sitting room, where he found her curled up in her blankets on the sofa. She made no move to greet him but he was in no mood to show her kindness either.

"You're making a mistake. You have so little faith in my ability that you would choose to kill yourself to end her?"

Adalaide snorted. "You told me yourself in three thousand years you've never stopped her. Wasn't it your *only* mission? Jophiel's entire line has been killed on your watch, apart from me and your sons."

The words cut deep, curbing some of his anger. Perhaps her actions weren't as coerced as he had assumed. Still, it seemed Dina had shared more of the story than was necessary. It was likely neither of them had faith in him.

"And who will care for our sons when you are in Alaxia?"

"I wouldn't dare ask you."

"Why are you angry with me? I sought to end her, to give you this mortal life with Henry and John. How am I the villain in this?" The leash he'd been attempting to hold on to his anger snapped, all the rage he'd felt the moment his chest spasmed, telling him of her foolish plan rushing back.

"You promised me you wouldn't leave me alone again!" she said, sitting up. The blanket slid off her shoulder, revealing bare skin. Even that perfect creamy shoulder wasn't enough to stop the hurt and terror blazing through him.

If she felt it, she didn't show it. "You know nothing of what it means to have someone other than yourself to think of, to care for. I cannot race into the night to slay beasts and demons. I must be here to care for the children who cannot care for themselves. When Jophiel told me of a way to keep them safe, I took it. I will not apologize for that."

Gabriel ground his teeth. "I will stop this." He said the words too quietly, but she heard.

"Go then, be a hero. It's your one talent." She slumped back in her seat, looking away from him.

He turned, shoulders squaring, paused, and considered turning back. He hadn't come intent on fighting. He hadn't planned to leave things this way, but the sparse emotions slipping through her wall between them were disappointment and regret. Regret was the one that stung the most. As he had expected, she had come to regret being tethered to him in the end.

He became dust, letting a phantom breeze carry him out of her home and into the night. Drifting along the Thames, he retraced Sanura's path from that first night. He had one week to stop this before meeting with the Fallen. If he could end her now, it would all be avoided

CHAPTER 37

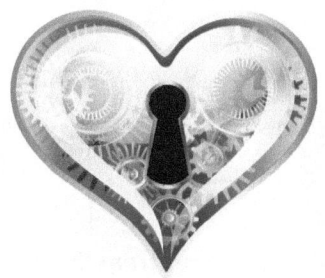

Adalaide

Henry's shrill cry made her wince. There were definite downsides to her abilities as a reash, her sharpened senses being one of them. She stepped into the room and was assaulted by a smell that could bring a sailor to tears.

"Poor thing," she crooned.

Holding her breath, she moved into the room and picked up the babe.

"Adalaide," Jophiel said behind her, making her jump.

She whirled around, holding her child to her chest. "You startled me."

"Apologies. I come with news."

Adalaide moved past her, carrying Henry to the bathing room to rinse him clean. John sniffled and began to wail. "Would you mind?" She tossed her chin toward the baby, who had noticed his brother's absence.

Jophiel nodded, moving to pick up the infant and cradle him in her arms. "He is hungry," she told Adalaide.

"He will have to wait. His brother has made a mess of himself. What is your news?"

"Gabriel will meet with the Fallen three nights hence."

Adalaide darted a dark glance at Jophiel. "You can't stop him?"

Jophiel gave her a look that asked if she had truly meant that question. No, she supposed she hadn't. Asking Gabriel to do anything was laughable. She chewed on her bottom lip, turning the faucet and holding out a wrist to test the water's temperature. "Will you go with him?"

Jophiel shook her head. "We are not on speaking terms at present."

Adalaide knew the feeling. "Perhaps you could send Raphael or another?"

"He is bringing Sariel."

"I don't believe I've heard of that one," Adalaide said lightly.

"His obligation keeps him quite apart from the rest of us."

Adalaide wasn't sure what that meant, but she wasn't sure what many things Jophiel said meant, so she nodded. "At least he will not be alone."

"He goes to bargain for your release from the spell."

Adalaide's nose crinkled. "What does the Fallen have to do with our spell?"

Jophiel looked down at the baby in her arms.

"Jophi?"

Jophiel said nothing.

"Jophiel, what haven't you told me?"

Jophiel's wings twitched, and her glow dimmed.

Adalaide finished pinning a new cloth on Henry and wrapped him in a light blanket, setting him down in her lap.

"Jophiel."

The angel looked up, her eyes mournful. "Magic which requires a life sacrifice belongs to the Fallen."

Adalaide stood, holding Henry out to Jophiel. She took him, passing John to her. She slid her nightgown over her shoulder and fed the baby, letting him nuzzle her chilled flesh.

"I think you had better explain yourself," she said, leaving the bathing room to return to the babies' nursery. She sat in a chair and rocked him as he drank.

"He won't accomplish anything by it. The magic may feed the Fallen, but he cannot change it."

Adalaide pursed her lips. What did that mean? What did any of it mean, and what could be done about it now? The bargain was struck. When the trap was laid and Sanura caught within it, Adalaide would have to die, feeding her life's blood into the spell to ensure Sanura was truly banished from the Earth forever.

She couldn't focus on that now. Not when all that mattered were the twins. "We must begin preparing for John and Henry's care when I'm gone," she said.

"They will have me and their father..." Jopheil's words trailed off.

"Precisely. Angels with more to do than care for humans and no concept of time are not the proper guardians for infants."

Jophiel grimaced and dipped her head. "What did you have in mind?"

"Although my sacrifice will ensure Sanura is trapped in Sheol, her creatures and the demons who roam the Earth will still be here, and I have no doubt they will seek to finish what she started. I have a distant cousin by marriage, unrelated to your line, with whom I have made enquiries. I hope to hear from her within the week.

"Now, tell me the rest of what we must do to ensure the spell succeeds."

When Jophiel had gone and Henry and John were safely tucked in their bassinet, Adalaide pulled out her father's journal and turned to a blank page. She'd read over many of his notes on the history of her family line and what they had done to Sanura.

The blood of one, the lives of many, must endure. Speak the words, know thyself true, or be damned. Flame of desire, gilded heart, protect what lies within. This Grave responsibility.

She huffed a laugh, recalling the times she had puzzled over those words. It was not until Jophiel had told her the story of Helena that she finally understood its meaning. It also clarified some of the calculations and alchemical compounds written into the earliest pages of the book.

Someone had carefully diagramed the various uses of metals in magical spells. The particular composition of the gold encapsulating Sanura's bone amplified the magic while also cloaking it from those who would seek to use it for harm.

A rather brilliant use of science in conjunction with magic. She wondered what future technological advances might come about as a result of her family's experiments.

Touching her pen to the page, she began to write.

A soul's great solace, recognizing an analogous umbra.

It comes in the night, threatening all I love.

She chewed her bottom lip. What could she say to explain to her sons the reason they had lost their mother? She continued writing.

It whispers in the dark, promising life evermore.

Myne immolation or oblation? Shall it be as it was meant, or do fates so entwined defy predestination?

She pressed the ivory end of her pen to her lip, wondering fleetingly if she had been wrong to make this choice. What if her slate hadn't been wiped clean? What if she wouldn't find him in the afterlife? Dismissing the thought, she continued writing.

When it finds you, be not swayed by dark desires or misdeeds. Stay the path of right. Know you this: actions are weighed, punishment meted out.

Her heart constricted, hoping her words would be clear enough when their paths crossed with the demons of this world.

My boys, should you find this one day and ask yourselves what became of your dear mother, know you were loved. You were loved beyond anything a mortal might comprehend.

Though our paths diverge from here, know there is a place beyond in which we shall see each other once more. Look after one another.

She blinked back a single tear. Were there words to explain why she was leaving them? Why she had given herself so they and everyone else would be safe. She pressed her pen to the page.

Five and twenty, the price I paid. Recompense for pneuma, I wolde gladly pay again. AG.

She read over the words, wishing she could more eloquently put to paper what she felt, why she had done it, and what she could tell them to keep them safe from the dangers they wouldn't know were there. Then, dipping her ink in the well once more, she pressed the tip of the pen to the page and added:

And if you should chance an encounter with your father, go easy on him.

She closed the journal, tears spilling down her cheeks. Had she been too hard on him? He fought for all souls. It was easy to forget that. To forget how important his task was. It was a further reminder of why she must unburden him of this one thing.

CHAPTER 38

Gabriel

Gabriel landed just inside the crumbling pillars of Pergamum and glanced to his left as Sariel landed beside him. He nodded, and Sariel nodded back.

It was one of only six places the Fallen could ascend to on Earth, thanks to the treaty he had agreed to all those years ago. Pergamum, once built as a temple to the pagan gods of ancient Greece, had been repurposed by a ruler named Trajan, a self-proclaimed god who traded his soul for power on Earth.

His deal, made before Samael was banned from setting foot on mortal soil, was made with the Fallen himself and created a loophole of sorts, allowing him to access the plane for short periods and only when encapsulated in a willing mortal body.

It was in just such a body he appeared now, lounging on a throne built on the backs of men several thousand years ago.

He stood, stretching out the ill-fitting human's skin, and cracked his neck. "Brothers! Just the two I have been missing," he said, strolling toward them.

Astaroth appeared on his left, and Paimon materialized on his right, swinging a vicious barbed tail behind her.

Samael rolled his human eyes. "Give me space, I beg you." He gave Gabriel and Sariel a knowing look as if they could relate.

Gabriel widened his stance, tightening his grip around his spear.

Samael halted just before them, looking up at their massive forms. He cupped his hands around his mouth. "Hullo up there, can you hear me?"

Gabriel ground his teeth. Even before he had fallen, Samael wasn't humorous, but he'd always fancied himself a comedian. He shrunk, reducing to the size of a man, and Sariel followed suit.

He had not spoken to Samael in some six thousand years. Somehow, he had not missed this.

"I come on behalf of—"

Samael waved a hand. "Yes, yes, your soul-bonded mate. Congratulations, brother. It is about time. I understand she dabbled with a bit of dark magic."

Gabriel's teeth sliced over his tongue, and he let the taste of his own blood calm his flaring anger. "She was coerced."

"By one of mine?"

When Gabriel said nothing, Samael clapped his hands together. "By one of our siblings?" He chuckled. "Let me guess. Was it dear Raphi? No. No. Someone more meddlesome." His eyes lit with dark amusement. "Dina."

Gabriel's brows dipped low on his forehead as a growl escaped his lips. "Enough games, Samael. I am willing to make a trade if you will undo the magic."

Samael raised a dark human brow and crossed his arms over his chest. "Go on."

"I will trade you the Lance of Lazarus."

At this, Sariel stepped forward. "He will not! I will not."

Gabriel glanced to his left at his brother, who had pulled a long sword from its sheath and held it out.

Astaroth and Paimon dived for him, misting in and out of solid form as they dodged his blade. Sariel struck Paimon through the chest, and she screamed before disappearing. Only within this place between realms was it safe for their souls to do battle in such a way, allowing a seraph to strike before receiving a blow.

Astaroth circled, diving once more. Sariel lunged for him just as he evaporated, only to appear again behind Sariel.

"Enough," Samael said in a cool voice. Both demon and seraph froze. Samael no longer held the power to freeze time, but he could spin it backward.

Gabriel watched Sariel pull his sword from Paimon as she solidified in front of him. Time moved forward again, but this time, Paimon dematerialized before he could strike and swung her long spiked tail, catching him in the back.

He fell to the floor, groaning, and Gabriel fell beside him, pressing a hand to his wound.

Sariel reached for a leather strap bisecting his chest and pulled Gabriel close. "You cannot bargain with the lance. It would mean the end for any he used it on. No soulmate is worth that."

Gabriel shook him off, pulling the last of the poison from Sariel's wound and standing. "I will retrieve it for you if you reverse the spell."

Astaroth and Paimon fell back, flanking Samael once more. "I cannot deny it's tempting, but what you ask is not mine to give."

Sariel got to his feet. "Nor is the lance Gabriel's to offer."

Gabriel tossed him a dark glare. Sariel only glared back.

"Very well. If you refuse me, I have no other business with you." Gabriel took a step back, preparing to leave.

"Ah, but there is another matter," Samael said.

Gabriel stopped.

"That nasty bit of magic you used." He directed this over Gabriel's shoulder to Dina, whom Gabriel had not seen appear behind him with Raphael. "It did have an unintended consequence."

This time, it was Dina who said, "What do you speak of?"

"It seems your blood sacrifice required an end to the entire line."

Gabriel's throat dried, and he swiveled his head to Dina, staring daggers at her.

"That's right. Your sweet Adalaide gave her life a little too willingly when she colluded to trap my mate in Sheol. The magic demands more." Samael raised a stiff gray brow. "One life to seal the fate of my mate for eternity from her other half? Did you think it would be enough?"

Gabriel fell to one knee, prepared to beg. Damn the consequences. This was more than he could bear.

"Stand, brother, you make yourself appear weak. I offer a solution."

The cold terror shooting down his spine diminished. "What do you want for their lives?"

"It's not just your children who must pay; it's the entire line, as the words to the spell demand."

"No," Dina cried. "You wouldn't."

"They will die at the same age Adalaide will; each one. Should she accomplish her goal, when she dies, she marks the death date of every member of her line. They will live long enough to procreate, and then, they too will die. It will continue for as long as one member of your wretched line continues to breed."

"Please," Gabriel breathed.

Samael tsked. "Be glad she was an adult when she cast this spell. Twenty-five is a long life for the creatures. Plenty of time for life experiences and all that. They get to live, and then they get to be with the other souls in Alaxia. If they deserve that end, of course. There are so many vices to lead them from their path." Samael pressed a finger to his human lip. "Well, I have plenty to keep them occupied below, should it be their destination."

A growl slipped past Gabriel's lips before he could swallow it back.

Samael laughed, a throaty sound he choked on at the end as if his lungs were not accustomed to making it.

"Name your price to free my sons of this curse."

Samael gave his wispy wraith companions a look. They chortled in dark amusement.

"Rise, Gabriel. Let us speak as brothers."

Gabriel stood, meeting Samael's dark stare.

Samael gazed into his eyes for a long moment, searching. At last, his crimson eyes widened, and his lips stretched into a cruel smile. "To free your sons of their curse, I ask only two things."

"Speak them."

"First," Samael held up a finger. "You or any of our brethren will never see your sons again. They must be raised in the absence of knowledge of our kind. When they die, their souls will pass on and rest as human souls in whichever realm they're deemed fit for."

"And the second?" Gabriel bit out, careful to give nothing that could be construed as an answer before the terms were laid out.

"And to release them from the curse your sibling placed them under," Samael shot a dark look at Dina, "you must give me your fire magic."

"Don't," Dina said, moving up behind Gabriel.

Gabriel spared her a glance but returned his focus to Samael. "If I agree to these terms, you will remove the curse that binds them to an early death?"

He swallowed sharp words resting heavily on his tongue, wishing there was any way to make this deal for his other half, but Samael would never agree to such a thing. He replayed the words in his mind, ensuring no loose threads could be unstrung.

"Yes."

Gabriel nodded once.

"Gabriel, we can find another way," Dina said, pressing against his wings.

"You've done enough, don't you think?" The words silenced her.

"You have a deal," he said, stretching a hand out to the Fallen.

Samael clasped it, digging sharp talons that grew unnaturally from the human's fingers into Gabriel's arm to draw golden blood. Lightning streaked overhead as Samael said, "And though you didn't ask it, I'll extend the same gift to *all* the men in your line."

Thunder clapped as the sky went black and streaks of red rained down upon them.

Gabriel tore his hand free. "What do you mean? We made a deal to end the curse. My sons will not pay for it."

"Agreed." Samael's teeth gleamed as another bolt of lightning streaked across the sky. "But the curse was on the entire line, and you only bargained for your sons. I did you a kindness. Only the women will pay for Adalaide's course."

"You tricked me." Gabriel lifted his spear, running a finger along its sharp tip. Nothing happened. He touched the metal once more.

Samael let out a bellowing laugh that seemed to rattle the very ground. He raised both hands as blue flame licked down his arms and ran along his fingers. His laugh grew, and the seraphim all stared in horror. A dark ripple of flame ran over blue, changing his flame as it went, to a deep crimson that was nearly black.

Inky sludge dripped from the man's nose, and a shape formed, hovering just off the ground before them. He let his form grow, and the flame ran up the length of his arms, cresting over dark, jagged horns.

"Run!" Gabriel shouted, and they dashed out of the ruins of Pergamum as arrows of crimson flame shot for their wings. When they breached the line, they blinked out of existence.

Gabriel landed at the edge of Alaxia and dropped to his knees, head in his hands. Someone laid a hand on his shoulder, but he shook it off. He hadn't the strength to fight anyone at the moment. She would die, and so would every woman in her line.

It was reckless, dangerous magic they played with, and Adalaide would pay the price for it.

When he had screamed his rage into the void of space, he lifted himself slowly from the gilded ground and trudged to the end of the hall.

"Aniel," he rasped.

The seraph looked up from a book and, upon seeing his wretched state, stood and hurried to the door. His mouth turned down at the corners, clasping Gabriel's forearm before ushering him inside.

Gabriel sat in the chair across from him and, after a long silence, said, "She will never forgive me."

He looked up, meeting his brother's eyes. There was pain and understanding in them. "I tried to protect her. I tried to do what was right, but she will die. When she does, she may not choose me a second time."

And his sons would live, but he would never see them again. An empty foreboding filled him, a portent of what was to come.

A warm hand rested on his knee, and he looked up. Aniel touched his chest, then pressed a hand to his own and nodded.

"Have faith?"

Aniel nodded.

It was humbling to sit with another who had been without his other half for so long and know he still had not given up hope. Or perhaps it was merely faith. A belief that, as Dina had said, all would be as it was meant to be.

He stood, clasping Aniel's forearms. "Thank you, brother."

He left, turning from the room to find Dina.

CHAPTER 39

Adalaide

Adalaide paced her foyer, staring at the grandfather clock in the hall.

Dina had promised to go with him even though he hadn't wanted her there. Now, it was half past one, and she had seen no one—not Dina, not Gabriel, not a single one of the angel bastards.

Was she meant to wait forever? To sit in her home and wait to see if they had died? Did angels die? Could they be killed by the devil? She stomped her foot on the ground.

Blessedly, the boys had gone down without a fuss and were sleeping peacefully. She went to her room, sliding open the window to feel the warm night air on her face.

Her birthday had come and gone, and she had turned twenty-five with no one being the wiser. Dina had said they would set specific parameters which would dictate how the spell worked. Her Latin was rubbish, so she understood very little of the actual spell, but the gist was that she must die, Sanura must be present, and Adalaide must be twenty-five.

There were other factors, ones she didn't understand, but those were the important bits. And she had turned twenty-five six days ago. It suddenly felt as though her life was a countdown clock ticking toward her end.

She wasn't ready. Her babies weren't yet four months. She hadn't heard their first words, seen them take their first steps, or watched them grow into the men they would become.

She leaned out the window, looking down, then up. Why was she always made to wait while they came and went as they pleased? She was through waiting.

Sending a blast of air beneath her feet, she angled herself out the window and shot up to the roof. There, she stared up at the expansive night sky and screamed for someone to answer her.

She was met with only the buzz of crickets and noises on the street below. "Come down here and answer me!" she shouted.

It was reckless and dumb, but perhaps all she needed was a bit of faith. Deciding, she backed up to the corner of her rooftop and ran, taking a flying leap, thinking: *Gabriel, I will find you in Alaxia, and there will be no more hiding from me.*

Her feet left the ground, and she was speeding up, up, into the sky. She fell again just as quickly, landing on the same rooftop. But it wasn't *her* roof. It was bright and shimmered in gold. A pair of massive gates were secured before her, and beyond them, a gleaming castle, larger than she could have ever dreamed, sparkled in an unnatural light.

A massive glowing man landed before the gates and swung a sword in her face.

She danced back, narrowly avoiding the slice of a razor-sharp blade, and threw up a hand, marveling at the blue flame that burst free, even here.

The golden-haired angel lowered his sword. "You are Gabriel's Naphil," he said.

She bristled at the possession he placed on her. "I am no one's anything," she said.

"I shall fetch Gabriel, one moment." He disappeared without waiting for her reply.

She spun in a circle, taking in the space. It was beautiful, to be sure, but it was lacking *something*. It certainly wasn't how she imagined the afterlife.

Jophiel appeared before her, followed by Gabriel, whose dark eyes promised murder.

Jophiel rushed forward, embracing her. "Are you well? Are you injured?"

"I was awaiting news." Adalaide leveled them both with stares. Gabriel was still glaring daggers at Jophiel, who seemed to be doing her best to avoid his gaze. "You never came back. I thought something happened to you."

"To us?" Jophiel gave a nervous laugh. "We're immortal. What could have happened to us?"

Gabriel shoved past his sister, getting between them. "Tell her what you've done, Dina."

Jophiel darted another nervous glance between them and opened her mouth. No words came out.

"What?" Adalaide asked, her throat going dry.

"Tell her," he growled.

Jophiel nodded, her wings twitching in agitation. "We met with the Fallen and learned—" she shot another nervous glance at Gabriel. "There's no easy way to put it."

"Tell me, Jophi," Adalaide said, scooting left to move around Gabriel. He went with her, blocking her path.

Jophiel's glow dimmed so much that she might have passed for human as she said, "We learned that... when you die... it will not be enough."

Adalaide rolled the words over in her mind. "Meaning?" she prompted.

"Meaning... There must be an end to my line."

"But, I have sons?" Adalaide's gaze darted to Gabriel. "Gabriel. What does she mean?"

Jophiel rushed on. "The women of our line will all die at the same age you do."

Adalaide processed her words, her hand flying to her mouth. "No."

Jophiel moved behind Gabriel, and his eyes narrowed on his sibling as she said, "It was the only way to stop her."

Adalaide stepped forward, baring her teeth. "I gave up everything for you, and you ask more of me?"

Gabriel spun around, grabbing her shoulders, a feral rage dancing in his eyes that she'd never seen before. "Do you think we ask this of you lightly? The fate of humanity rests with you. We ask a lot. Too much. If you weren't so selfless, it would have been simpler."

She scoffed, wrenching free of his hold. "If I were more wicked, my kin would suffer less?"

Gabriel stepped back, his wings stretching behind him as his words came out sharp and accusing. "I did not ask you to agree to this. You made the sacrifice, and I cannot help you now."

The words cut deep and her shoulders slumped as she dropped her gaze to the floor. "It's my family," she whispered.

"Only the women. This much I could do for you." He leaned forward some of his anger banking as he wiped a tear from her cheek. "Human lives are brief. You will see that much awaits you once yours has ended."

She batted his hand away, stepping back.

"You've all but ensured that, have you not? I will not see my boys grow up. I will not see the men they will become."

"You *will* see them again."

Another tear slid down her cheek. Gabriel reached for her, but she continued backward until she was at the pearly gates, and then she was falling.

She landed hard on the roof of her building, a sharp pain piercing through her, making her gag. She dropped to her knees and retched, the contents of her dinner spilling over the rooftop. She rubbed her chest, taking short, gasping breaths.

It was the bond, rebelling against her departure. Was that how he felt every time he left? It was agony. And he had left so many times.

A piercing screech rent the air, and even through layers of brick, she could hear Henry's cry. Taking a running jump, she leapt off the edge, palms facing down, and, using air magic, navigated into her bedroom window.

In the babies' room, she let out a sigh when she found them wrestling each other in their bassinet. She picked them up, nestling one in each arm, and hummed softly to them as she swallowed around the slowly receding pain in her heart.

Her chest gave a warm spasm as the ember glowed in recognition of its twin's arrival. It was sweet relief from the pain of leaving him, but she squeezed her eyes shut, drawing up those mental shields Jophiel had taught her to erect, and took a few calming breaths.

She didn't have time to fight with him—or any of them. She was a mother now, and two precious beings relied on her. How had she been so short-sighted?

Sacrificing herself for the angels when it meant her line would pay the price forever?

"I never wanted this for you," his deep rumbling voice said from the doorway, making her toes curl.

She wanted to hate him, to blame him, but it wasn't his fault. She had been so desperate to find a way to prove herself worthy of an eternity in Alaxia that she would have agreed to anything.

She was upset because *she* had been a fool.

Gabriel crossed the room, settling himself beside her on the bed. He gave her no room to move away.

Wedged between him and the boys, she huffed, turning her back to him.

"Light."

"Don't call me that."

He leaned across her twisted form, settling two fingers under her chin and turned her face to his. "You're no fool. You're the bravest human, the bravest being I've ever known."

She tore her chin from his grasp, swiping a tear from her cheek.

"I've doomed my entire line."

"Only the women." He repeated the words from before.

She hadn't missed the way he hadn't greeted their boys, though. The way he hadn't scooped them up or cooed over them. He hadn't so much as glanced their way. He was disappointed in her choice. In her.

"If you can survive beyond twenty-five, we can avoid this curse altogether," he said.

She turned back to him, hope shining in her. "Do you believe that would work?"

"Yes."

The pain she had not yet let herself drown in was draining away, replaced with something new. It gleamed, scouring the dark places in her mind. She could survive to twenty-six and avoid cursing her line.

They would find another way to end Sanura.

She twisted toward him, wrapping him in a fierce hug. "Together, we'll face it together."

He stiffened in her grasp.

Some of the warmth in her bled away as the inkling of premonition that always guided her told her she was about to be dealt another blow. She loosened her grip, leaning back to meet his stare.

His eyes never wavered from hers, never looked to the squirming babies beside her as he told her what he had done to protect their sons.

Her hand flew to her mouth. "No. No. You can't."

"If there's even the slightest chance you don't survive to twenty-six, it will have been for nothing if I don't keep up my end of the deal. I cannot be here."

His eyes were brimming with sorrow, and she heard the unspoken words. It was killing him not to look at them, to hold them, to know he would be giving them up for the rest of their lives.

"Only until we beat this," he said aloud.

One year. She'd done it before. She could do it again. She let her mental shields drop, showing him her confidence in their plan. In him.

"My light in the darkness, I don't want to leave you. I never want to be parted."

She rolled her eyes. "You're hardly here. It will be a greater inconvenience for me by far."

He smiled, but it didn't reach his eyes. "Stay alive. Promise me."

"We're rubbish at promises," she reminded him.

The dark swirls in his eyes seemed to intensify and he leaned in, pressing a soft kiss to her lips. She opened her mouth, sucking his lower lip between her teeth and bit.

He grinned. *My perfect match,* he said into her mind.

My stubborn soulmate, she said back.

She released his lip from between her teeth and they kissed, his golden blood mingling with their tongues.

Then, as if she'd dreamed it, he was gone; only sparkling bits of dust glinted in the moonlight, catching in her hair before they flew out the window.

CHAPTER 40

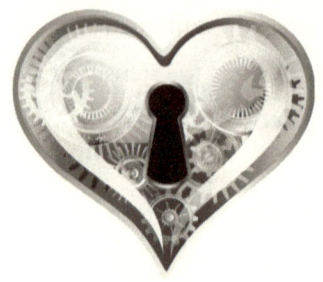

Adalaide

It was July. The boys had celebrated six months of life, and Adalaide had celebrated two months of being twenty-five.

Her chest ached every time she thought of him, but every now and then, he sent sweet thoughts into her mind. Whenever she was having a particularly rough day, her chest buzzed, letting her know he was nearby.

Henry could say *aglll,* which she had translated to mean angel, and she melted every time he said it.

She'd had relatively few attacks, which should have made her feel better, but instead, their infrequency made her increasingly wary. Sanura was planning something.

After all, Adalaide could die, but if they didn't perform the other steps in the spell, Sanura wouldn't be affected by it. It made the most sense that she would send someone else to end Adalaide and her boys.

"Ada."

Adalaide froze, dropping the towel she had been folding into her basket and turned slowly.

"You have some nerve, showing your face."

Jophiel held up her hands in a placating gesture. "I know you're upset."

"You have no idea how upset I am."

"I never meant for any of this to happen."

"You never meant to curse your entire line to put an end to a necromancer who is the soulmate of the devil and a thorn in your side?" She propped a hand on her hip.

"I want to end her. I won't deny it."

Adalaide waited for the angel to say more. When Jophiel said nothing, she asked, "Why are you here?"

"I want you to reconsider."

Adalaide snorted. "Reconsider cursing my line?"

"It's my line, too. You're all my children, but she must be stopped. Only my line can do it."

Adalaide chewed her bottom lip. "Gabriel is hunting her. He *will* stop her."

"If she survives beyond your twenty-sixth birthday, if he's unsuccessful, she will be unkillable."

Adalaide crossed her arms over her chest. "I will not be your experiment. My sons need me."

"She continues to build her army. Imagine the world you're leaving to them with her in it. Already, more than a thousand of the nasdaqu-ush are converging on America. They have the ability to wipe an entire continent clear of its inhabitants, but you could stop it."

Adalaide glanced at her boys, biting down hard on her lower lip. "I can't. They need me."

Jophiel crossed the room, laying a hand on Adalaide's shoulders. "Your cousin would care for them. Who will care for the rest of the world when Sanura's army is so great even the seraphim cannot stop her?"

She sent a thought to Gabriel, willing him to come, to help her fight this battle. He was silent. Somewhere too far away to hear her.

Jophiel's eyes met hers. "He is fighting, but even he cannot fight so many."

A jolt of fear shot through her. He was immortal, wasn't he? He couldn't be killed. That was what he had told her, but...

"I have a plan," Jophiel said.

Adalaide listened, shaking her head every time the plan became more absurd. "What makes you think she would fall for that?"

"The amulet is what she truly wants. It is the only thing keeping her from returning to her analogous umbra. She would do anything to reclaim it."

"She could send a demon."

"For a prize this great, she would come for it herself."

Adalaide stood, shaking out some of her nerves. Was she prepared to die? She had been before Gabriel had given her hope. But Jophiel was right. What world was she leaving for her sons when Sanura's army might soon overrun it?

"I'll take the boys to my cousin and give this one shot." She stared down her nose at the angel who was looking at her solemnly. "If it doesn't work, we will never speak of it again."

She packed her bags quickly, tucking the leather journal and the real amulet into a bag filled with the boy's things.

She packed their favorite stories, which she read to them each night, and the soft pink blanket they fought over while they listened. She loaded them into their bassinet and stuffed her overnight bag into a carriage, and they set off for Oxford.

When she safely deposited her sons in her cousin's care, giving her step-by-step instructions and explaining she would be back in a fortnight, she departed, feeling a wholly new kind of ache in her chest.

She hoped she would see her sweet boys again, but if she couldn't, she would leave the world a better place for them.

Hope had been reawoken in her, something she never dreamed she'd feel again.

CHAPTER 41

Gabriel

Gabriel grabbed his chest, sinking into the mud. Night-beings fell on him, biting and tearing, some ripping his wings. They were nothing. They were the biting of ants.

His chest had been torn in two. A deep, aching emptiness gutted him, just like the day half his soul had been torn from his body.

Chamuel, or one of his other siblings, pulled the nasdaqu-ush off him, yanking him up. Someone wrapped an arm around his waist, and then he was back in Alaxia, the pain receding but not gone.

Hands pressed to his wings, his neck, his back and arms.

He sucked in a sharp breath gasping as he sat up. Then he was running, running to the gates to welcome her, to claim her. He stopped just inside and watched, waiting for them to swing wide. Dina landed beside him.

The anger and pain he'd felt over her betrayal was replaced with such joy.

She was coming home. His light would be there soon.

Charmuel and Mary met them at the gates. A dozen others arrived, all circling him.

He glanced around nervously. What if she rejected him? What if she chose to rest with the human souls rather than remain with him in her seraph form?

He darted a nervous glance at Mary. "Where is Raphael?"

Her gaze slid to the gates where Raphael normally stood watch and back to him. "I am unsure."

Gabriel's fingers traced absently over his chest. The pain of her dying had been more terrible than he'd expected. A wrenching at their soul. Surely, their soul would have warmed at the prospect of completing the bond, of coming home.

His gaze trailed over the sea of siblings who had gathered and were now murmuring to one another.

"Uriel," he called.

Uriel came forward, sliding between wings as he made his way to the gate. "Brother," he said, clasping Gabriel's arm.

"What did it feel like when your other half passed from the Earthly plane?"

Uriel's brow furrowed. "Like my soul was coming home."

Something sharp stabbed through Gabriel. He turned to Chamuel. "And for you, brother?"

Chamuel cleared his throat, stepping forward. "Like the first rays of sun banishing the fog."

Gabriel pressed his fingers into that place in his chest where it had been solid moments ago. Now, it was a gaping chasm. Unbreachable. He could no easier have spanned the distance than he could press a hand to her cheek and feel the smooth skin beneath his fingers.

He looked to his sister. "Dina. Is she—" he choked on the words, unable to speak them.

Dina's swirling eyes went round. "No. It's not possible. I made her a reash. Her sins were wiped clean."

She was right. As a reash, she had been given a fresh start. Any misdeeds were erased. Unless... Unless she had committed new acts so unforgivable that she was bound for Primoria.

Raphael landed beside him, taking in the crowd. "What have I missed?"

Gabriel spun to him, eyes wild. "Where is she? Why is she not at the gates?"

Mary moved to her mate's side, resting a gentle hand on Gabriel's shoulder. "She may yet arrive."

He flinched out of her touch, spreading his wings wide and several of his siblings moved back, giving him space.

He launched over the gates and fell, dropping to the Earth.

Landing outside her door, he pushed in. Dizzying pain hit him hard, and he sagged into the wall, catching his breath. Where it had been aching hollowness in Alaxia, here it was the rending of his very being, hollowing him with such force he staggered to his knees, tearing at the pain in his chest.

A line of dark crimson trailed across the floor. He crawled toward it, pulling himself into the sitting room and letting out a mournful howl as he fell beside her lifeless form.

She was ashen and already cooling under his touch. Her bright blue eyes were wide, staring at nothing, and the pentagram in the middle of the floor was drenched in her blood.

He lay down beside her, pressing his forehead to her cool cheek.

He had known she was gone, felt it at the core of his being, but finding her there, devoid of life and love and their soul, tore something irreparable in him.

She was gone. And her soul was not with him.

Curling himself over her still form, he wrapped his wings over them both and blocked out the garish light, too bright for a world that no longer held her in it.

It had been a week or a month. The unbearable light refracting off every surface in his room never changed, never dulled.

He blinked up at Aniel's somber face. When he blinked again, it was Michael.

The next time he opened his eyes, Dina was there. He couldn't muster the energy to be angry with her, to feel anything.

"Don't know why she isn't here," Dina was saying, the words finally penetrating some of the haze in his mind.

"*He* has her." His voice was scratchy from disuse.

"Who? Do you know where she is? We've been searching but have found no trace," Camael said.

"She can be in but one place," Dina said softly.

"Let's get her," Camael said.

Dina rested a hand on Gabriel's cheek. "Will you go with us, brother?"

The words sank in. He nodded slowly. *Yes. Yes!* More of the fog cleared. He would go, and he would bargain for her return.

CHAPTER 42

Gabriel

"Please," he begged. "Please give her back to me."

"If I but had her to give, brother."

Gabriel fell to his knees, dropping his head until it touched the Earth. "Name your price."

Samael's low chuckle reverberated through the cavernous space. "I would never dare ask how you'll suffer eternity in such a state. For I may well be the only other who knows your pain."

Gabriel raised his head. "This is punishment for your mate's banishment? I had no hand in it. You know that."

"Brother," Samael cooed. "You misunderstand. I seek to offer my condolences from one separated from his mate to another. We are kindred in this."

"Give her to Alaxia. Let her soul rest."

"I swear," Samael crossed his fingers over his chest, "I would return her this instant, no price asked if she were in my realm. But she is not."

Gabriel bowed his head once more. The forked tongue slithering over the Fallen's lips—a reminder of his dishonesty—meant he could be lying, but the words tasted of truth. If not in Primoria and not in Alaxia, where?

He rose slowly, tucking his wings tightly behind him. Dina and Camael moved closer, guarding his back.

"What if I could get Sanura back? Would you give her to me then?"

Camael and Dina both hissed sharp reprimands at his back.

Samael's gaze fell heavily on Dina and Camael, then slid back to him.

"Do you have her to give?"

Gabriel opened his mouth... to lie. He closed it, shaking his head.

Samael gave him a dismissive wave of the hand and turned, striding away from them. "You waste my time. Come back when you have something to offer."

"Me," he whispered.

Samael laughed derisively. "In this state, your soul is worth nothing to me. Leave and do not request a meeting again."

Dina slid her arm through Gabriel's, pulling him back. "Come, brother. He doesn't have her."

His feet moved leadenly away, dragging as he went.

Dina and Camael prepared for ascent. When she saw him rooted to the spot, she wrapped an arm around him.

"Don't," he said, desolation lacing his words."I want to stay on the mortal plane for a time."

"The suffering will be too great here; come home." Dina's words were soft, but the aching hole in his chest was akin to the pain in his soul, and he yearned to revel in it.

She shook her head. Camael took a step toward him, but she pulled him back, and they were gone.

When he was alone, he gazed up at the moonless sky, spotting the dusting of stars that made up the Taurus constellation.

He had been so certain her freckles were a sign of something greater. Had it always been about Sanura? It didn't matter anymore. Nothing did. He was alone, and she was lost to him forever.

Gabriel sat back in his golden chair, thinking nothing. Feeling nothing.

One year became ten; ten became fifty; they continued on. He stared into the empty hearth and prayed Adalaide would return.

A knock at the door roused him from some thought—a memory of her laugh.

"Henry has come home," Dina said in the doorway. He nodded. "Will you come see him?"

Henry had lived more than sixty years. A long life for most humans and a good one if he'd ended up here.

He shook his head. "Not today."

Dina hovered at the edge of the entrance to his room, but she didn't step in.

When she'd gone, he resumed staring at nothing, falling back into the memory he'd been lost in. He brushed a dark curl back from her face, blinded by the radiant smile she gave to only him and in it, knew he was forgiven. She touched his face, soft fingers tracing the dimple in his cheek and that gaping hollow space in his chest was filled with the memory of his perfect mate.

If he could have done it all over. He would have protected her, shielded her from his world and everything that came with it. She would have never known what awaited her if they bonded, and at the end of her long human life, she would have rested with the humans, never having to choose between her life and humanity.

Sometime later, it could have been weeks or years, Chamuel stopped in his door. "We need you. The human world is at war, and demons threaten to overturn it."

When he looked up, Chamuel was gone.

Something stirred in his chest. It wasn't hope. Hope had died long before now. He peered into the hall, hearing voices.

He stepped out as dozens of seraphim ran by. He thought to ask where they were going, but when he remembered, they were gone.

He was moving, but he didn't know where he was headed. When he stopped in front of it, he understood. It gleamed in the opalescent light of Alaxia. He'd been in this state so long; it was the only reason he hadn't arrived at this conclusion sooner.

There was nothing left for him.

He lifted the chalice, turned, and knelt before a gleaming fountain. Dipping the chalice, he filled the cup with golden liquid.

It was silent as a tomb in this place. A room where none ever came.

It was fitting that his broken soul would pulse for the last time in complete silent stillness. He would no longer disrupt the space he occupied; when his soul rested, it would be as if he had never existed.

He lifted the cup to his lips.

The feeling in his chest warmed again. A jolting sensation similar to that of earth magic when he breathed new life into being.

His soul pulsed once.

The cup clattered to the floor.

THE END

THANK YOU

Thank you for reading Light. If you enjoyed it, please consider leaving an honest review on your favorite site. If this is your first foray into the world of the Prophecies of Angels and Demons, consider starting at the beginning with Grave Secrets.

To read Grave Secrets and the entire Prophecies of Angels and Demons series on Amazon

To leave a review for Light on Amazon

To leave a review for Light on Goodreads

Sign up for my newsletter for discounts & to stay up to date on everything I'm working on

ACKNOWLEDGMENTS

If you've made it this far and kept reading, a special thank-you to you. Readers like you give me the courage to keep writing and keep telling my characters' stories. If you loved this novella, please consider leaving a review. Your words of encouragement are sometimes exactly what I needed to get through my day. This story was especially important to me because Gabriel holds a special place in my heart. I hope you loved it too!

To my mom, who continues to be my first reader, even the horrible first drafts, I'm so grateful our love of reading brought us even closer.

To my son, who tells everyone he meets about my books, sometimes to my embarrassment. Thank you for being my biggest supporter.

To my street team, for believing in me and being so willing to give your time and energy to share my stories with the world.

To Dawn Darling for making this awesome book cover, and being a great friend and sounding board.

To Michaela C for being such an amazing editor!

Thank you.